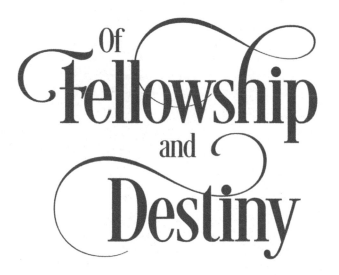

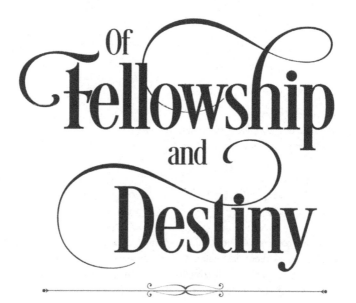

JUDY S. WAGNER

TABLE OF CONTENTS

DEDICATION:

"Of Fellowship and Destiny" is a fictional romance story which takes place in a small rural southern town in the state of Tennessee.

It speaks to the contributions a group of Catholic Christian volunteers make in their efforts to assist the poor and underprivileged church community to which they've been assigned.

It highlights certain challenges one of the coordinators faces throughout her outreach ministry, which ultimately leads to her destiny.

The novella's main character, "Elea" is a shortened version of the name "Eleanor". "Eleanor" loved to write. In her youth, she had dreams of one day becoming a writer of stage plays.

The author affectionately dedicates this story to her mother, "Eleanor".

ACKNOWLEDGEMENT

Thanks and Acknowledgements to the following people:

Husband Bill Wagner for his ongoing support of this endeavor

Brother-in-law Fred Wagner for reading the manuscript

Author and friend Susan Mellon for her ongoing relentless faith in me

Formatter and friend Andie Hansen for her amazing talents and patience

Graphic Designer and friend Brenda Walter for her beautiful cover designs

Blue Valley Author Services

CHAPTER 1

I T WAS ON A HOT, August day when social workers Scott Preston and Elea Johnson traveled the long, dusty dirt roads in Scott's SUV. Their destination was the Evangelical Community Church, located in Scarlet Oak Valley, Tennessee. Scott and Elea were Catholic outreach volunteer coordinators who were on a six-month mission to serve the church's underprivileged community. They had traveled for the past fourteen hours, having departed Metro Line City, New York the prior evening. The intense heat and humidity of the day took its toll on them. They pulled into a small luncheonette they spotted along the rural dirt road and stopped in for something to eat. There were only ceiling fans, but no air conditioning in the luncheonette. As they took seats, they chatted.

"It shouldn't be too much longer until we arrive," Scott remarked to Elea, "We have an appointment with the Reverend Dr. Everett Ward. We'll need to let him know our team of volunteers will be arriving tomorrow and will need to take instruction from him as to where he wants us to be stationed on their church grounds."

"I'm looking forward to this assignment, Scott, and really can't wait to get started," Elea responded with an enthusiastic smile.

They brushed off the crumbs from their table, asked for cold waters to go, departed the non-air conditioned luncheonette, got back into the SUV, and traveled onward. They continued to drive along the rural dirt roads. As they drove, Scott and Elea enjoyed the picturesque southern countryside with its fields of cows and other farm animals they passed along the way. They took note of the quaint country homes and the strong, sweet smell of honeysuckles. The slow, laid-back environment of the south was a far different cry from the area they had been used to. In Metro Line City, New York, the busy metropolis never slept.

One hour from the time they departed the luncheonette, they arrived in the small town of Scarlet Oak Valley and pulled up to the Evangelical Community Church.

Elea exclaimed, "Great timing, Scott, I can't believe we arrived here just in time for our appointment with the Reverend Dr. Ward. The directions provided were very accurate, but still you never can be sure of timing once you make it into these rural communities."

Scott smiled and replied, "You're absolutely right."

As they were exiting the SUV, briefcases in hand, a short, elderly, gray-haired, heavy-set gentleman dressed in a white suit opened the door of the small church, smiled and exclaimed, "Welcome to both of you! Please step inside to my office. I'm Everett Ward, the pastor of this church."

He continued to smile as he held the door open to allow Scott and Elea entrance. Once inside, Scott extended his hand, smiled and spoke, "Hello, Reverend Dr. Ward, this is Elea Johnson, my fellow outreach coordinator, and I'm Scott Preston."

Elea added, as she also extended her hand to him, "Very nice to meet you, Reverend Dr. Ward, and thank you for welcoming us!"

"Come in, come in, and let's step into my office and chat. And no need to be so formal. You may address me as 'Everett' if you'd like, or 'Reverend Ward', whichever you prefer. I'm afraid my secretary, Beth Leiden, has the day off, otherwise I would have introduced you. She's very efficient and helps keep a certain order to church business. Please know I'm very grateful you're here. Before we chat at length, have you eaten?" Reverend Ward asked, as he observed Scott and Elea and noticed they looked tired.

"Oh, we're fine, Reverend Ward, but thank you," Scott replied.

Reverend Ward sat behind his huge oak desk, while Scott and Elea took seats across from him. He shed his white suit jacket, rolled up his long sleeves, and then started to fan himself. There was no air conditioning in his office, and the summer heat and humidity level was high.

"So let's see if I have this right. The two of you are social workers and Catholic outreach coordinators from Metro Line City, New York. You'll be managing a group of volunteers who will be stationed at our church. You've been assigned by your diocese for a six-month assignment to help our church, while also assisting the general community. This is all part of an outreach program sponsored by the main organization, Catholic Volunteer Workers of America." Scott and Elea both nodded.

Elea added, "We're really excited and are looking forward to helping everyone." She explained, "Our volunteers will assist in whatever areas you may need us. Scott and I understand there's much work that needs to be done here in Scarlet Oak Valley, especially among the elderly, youth, and underprivileged in the community."

Scott explained, "If at the end of our six-month assignment, you feel the community still requires our assistance, we're happy to accommodate you. But if you don't require our assistance at the end of the six months, we volunteers would then move on to another location for the same purpose."

Reverend Ward was impressed, "Well, you both seem like very kind-hearted, compassionate people, and I thank you. Our small congregation could really use some wonderful workers to help in the many areas of this community. So when is your team of volunteers arriving?"

Just as Elea was ready to respond to his question, there was a knock on the door, with someone slowly starting to open it. He was a tall, serious-looking, very handsome, well-built man with piercing light green eyes and dark brown spiked hair. He was dressed in jeans and an opened flannel shirt, revealing a gray t-shirt. The first person he noticed as he entered Reverend Ward's office was Elea. He stared for a minute, seemingly surprised, and then glanced away from her. His eyes and attention then focused solely on Reverend Ward.

"Oh, Kyle, please come in. Actually, you should join our meeting. This is Mr. Scott Preston and Miss Elea Johnson. They're the two Catholic volunteer coordinators who will be managing workers who are going to serve the youth and elderly population within our church. In addition, they'll be accommodating those in most need of assistance in our community. We're really looking forward to welcoming them to fellowship with us. Miss Johnson, Mr. Preston, this is our associate pastor, Mr. Kyle Williams. Please have a seat, Kyle." Reverend Ward graciously welcomed him.

With one hand still on the open door, Kyle responded, "No thank you, I'll be leaving in just a minute. Beth's watching Jack and I need to get back home." He spoke those words with the same serious demeanor on his expressionless face. He paused, and then with a look of confusion asked, "Everett, shouldn't we be welcoming volunteers from our own southern Evangelical organization instead of from the Catholic camp up north?"

Elea glanced over at Scott in total shock. She couldn't believe what a rude statement the associate pastor made! For such a good looking man, he appeared somewhat arrogant. Scott returned her glance, seeming very surprised, as well.

Reverend Ward addressed his associate, "Kyle, I've already discussed everything with their diocese in New York. These coordinators and volunteers will take a six-month assignment here, and their assignment has also met with the approval of our senior board of deacons." He added, "Everything's been finalized, Kyle. You and your son were visiting your parents in Arkansas during the time when this was discussed with our congregation's hierarchy. The board unanimously agreed that our church could certainly use a great deal of help. This is a small community of poor people who are in dire need of assistance. And let's not forget the charitable projects we organize to benefit the nearby churches."

With that said, Kyle maintained his cynical demeanor, frowned, shook his head, let the door close, and departed. Scott and Elea sat quietly, having been made to feel both awkward and uncomfortable.

"I truly apologize for my associate's unkind words to both of you," Reverend Ward was obviously embarrassed.

"Oh, that's fine, please think nothing of it," Scott responded, and added, "I guess this was all new information to him."

Elea agreed, "We'll do the best we can, Reverend Ward, and are very much looking forward to getting to know the community and fellowshipping with your church's members."

"Great then, please allow me to show both of you the housing facility where you and your workers will be boarding throughout the time you'll be working with us."

Reverend Ward got up from his desk, and the three of them took a short walk. He led Scott and Elea to a large, old-looking white building located behind the parsonage.

Reverend Ward explained, "This building had previously been used to house the homeless members of our church, who, unfortunately, have all passed away. As the building serves no real purpose at this time, I informed your diocesan outreach director that you and your workers were free to take up residency in it throughout the time you'll be here. When you see the inside of this building, you'll agree it's very old and dated. It contains two large bedrooms, two standard-size bathrooms, a common area in the center of the building where you could hold your meetings, and a small kitchen area. I'm sure that you'll manage to make yourselves quite comfortable. I'll provide keys for you, which you may feel free to duplicate and distribute to your volunteers. Oh, you had asked the question of parking for when your volunteers arrive. Feel free to have everyones' vehicles park in the back of this building."

After ending their introductory meeting and thanking Reverend Ward, Scott and Elea grabbed their luggage out of the SUV, then went inside to unpack their bags. Since both were exhausted after their long commute, they immediately set up their aero beds in their designated rooms. They rested for about an hour.

Afterwards, they discovered a nearby diner, then briefly explored the surrounding area in Scott's SUV. Both were mainly interested in locations where grocery items could be purchased, hardware stores for home repairs, drug stores, doctors' offices, and other relevant places where supplies could be obtained for various building projects. They considered that these places would be of interest to the volunteers.

The following day, five sizeable SUVs, two persons per vehicle, arrived on the grounds of the small community church. Scott and Elea directed them as to where to park, and then requested everyone to immediately congregate for five minutes in front of the white building.

"Welcome, everyone, so happy you all made it here. Before Elea and I show you where you'll be boarding, let's have a quick meeting right here on the grounds." The workers stood as Elea passed out bottles of water to all of them.

Scott spoke, "This is Elea Johnson and I'm Scott Preston. We're the coordinators of the outreach program sponsored by Catholic Volunteer Workers, of which all of you are volunteers. Now if you turn to face the facility directly behind you, this will be your 'new home' for the entire duration of the time you'll be here. Elea and I had keys made for you. The women will use the large bedroom to the west side of the building and the men will use the other large bedroom located on the opposite side. Same with the two bathrooms. I assume all of you brought along your individual aero beds for sleeping. You'll be living 'dormitory' style. We'll refer to this building as the 'dorm'. Elea and I scoped it all out, and we have no doubt, that while space is tight, we'll all be comfortable here."

The excited volunteer workers nodded their heads as they sipped their waters, proceeded to unpack their vehicles, and filed into the dorm.

Judy S. Wagner

CHAPTER 2

SUNDAY MORNING ARRIVED. SCOTT, ELEA and their respective volunteers filed into the first pew of the Evangelical Community Church awaiting the start of services. As Elea gazed around the inside of the small building, she determined that this was a multi-aged, diverse congregation. There were also quite a few elderly members, as well.

Reverend Ward started the services by warmly greeting and welcoming everyone. Sitting on the opposite side on the altar was Kyle Williams, the associate pastor. He was dressed in his service vestments, frowning, appearing bored, and clearly acting like his time was being wasted.

Reverend Ward spoke, "Brothers and sisters, before we begin our prayer service this morning, may I kindly introduce everyone to our group of Catholic outreach volunteers from Metro Line City, New York. These volunteers will be working with our church and community for the next six months. The group is headed by Mr. Scott Preston and Miss Elea Johnson, the group's two coordinators. After services, we'll proceed downstairs to our fellowship hall, have some refreshments, and then Mr. Preston and Miss Johnson will explain in detail their outreach program. Now let us begin...."

After services, the congregation proceeded downstairs to the fellowship hall. Everyone helped themselves to coffee, tea, juice and refreshments that were available. Scott, Elea and their volunteers sat at a large, separate round table and waited patiently for Reverend Ward to introduce them.

On Reverend Ward's cue, Scott stood, approached the podium and proceeded to speak first. He introduced all ten of the volunteers who would be assisting. When Scott finished speaking, he introduced Elea, who would provide more specifics and respond to questions. She proceeded to speak more at length as to who their organization, Catholic Volunteers, was and how the outreach program benefitted the people of many underprivileged communities. Since she was such an eloquent speaker, she had the undivided attention of the small church's congregation.

As Elea scanned the room, Kyle, the associate pastor, walked in through the side door in the back of the hall, guiding a young male child, possibly seven or eight years of age. Elea noticed the child appeared shy and focused his head downward. They took seats in the very back of the hall, talked with each other and ignored her presentation. A tall, slender, attractive short-dark-haired woman then joined them. She and the associate pastor both sat with the young child in the middle between them. The woman, as well, ignored everything Elea was presenting.

After Elea's presentation, the volunteers began to socialize with church members, including Reverend Ward. Reverend Ward emphasized that various repairs needed to be made to the old church building itself. The building had long been neglected; and since the congregation was small, funds were low. Funds were allocated to this particular church from the main organization, but it looked obvious that the small church and community needed to host some fundraisers to supplement any additional costs for repairs.

An hour later, Elea and Scott loaned assistance to the church's Sunday hospitality committee in their clean-up efforts of fellowship hall, clearing food and drink off the tables and wiping them down.

As Elea was working, she overheard the tall woman who had sat with Kyle, the associate pastor, and the young child, say to a small group of women, "I have no idea what 'they're' doing here. Kyle doesn't understand it, either. There are enough of us here to help our church. They all need to go back up north from where they came."

Elea's heart raced. She took a deep breath, approached the group of women, smiled and spoke, "Hello ladies, I'm Elea Johnson. I assure you our group isn't out to take over your congregation. We were told there was a great need for assistance here at this church. We volunteers were sent here for the next six months for the purpose of helping to make a difference in this community."

The woman who had been speaking to the group of women folded her arms, frowned, and stared at Elea. Taking this woman's lead, her friends did likewise. None of the women were friendly. Elea stood awkwardly glancing around at their snobbish-looking, unrelenting faces.

Just then, Kyle, who had shed his service vestments, along with the young child who was with him, stopped where Elea was speaking to the women.

"Ladies," he greeted them, "Some kind of meeting going on here, Beth?" he asked as he faced the woman who had spoken to the group of her friends.

"I was just telling the ladies that you and I feel this Catholic group shouldn't be working here at our church, that we have enough workers to keep our church running, and that there should be plenty of work for them to be doing in the north."

Elea was really starting to feel unwelcome and out of place. She nervously faced Kyle, Beth, and the rest of the women, "Well, if you'd rather not have us, our intention is certainly not to make anyone uncomfortable with our presence. I'll speak to my fellow coordinator, Scott, and we'll let Reverend Ward know that we'll be moving on."

Kyle stared at her with a serious, fixed expression, then spoke, "No, don't go to Everett. He's obviously been looking forward to you and your volunteers serving the needs of our community, so keep him happy."

He added in a sarcastic tone and with a frown on his face, "I, personally, don't feel you all should be here, but what do I know, I'm just the associate pastor."

Elea faced everyone and sadly replied, "I'm sorry you feel that way."

No one said a word and just stared at her with blank expressions on their faces. Kyle then turned and led the young child out of the fellowship hall and beckoned Beth to join them. The group of women walked up the stairs, and Elea walked behind them. No one held the door for her as they all exited the building.

That evening back at the dorm, Elea discussed with Scott what had taken place and the cold, unfriendly reception she received after services.

"That was pretty rude of all of them," Scott replied, "It doesn't matter how 'they' feel; it's what their pastor wants that counts."

Elea responded, "I know, I just hope they don't try to make life too uncomfortable for us while we're here. And what is up with that associate pastor? He's a great looking guy, but he seems to have a real attitude. I noticed he had a young child with him."

Just then, a knock was heard on the door. Scott opened it. There stood a middle-aged, very friendly-looking woman holding a cake in a plastic carrier. She was short, overweight, had medium-length wavy blonde hair, blue eyes and a sweet friendly smile.

"Hi, I'm Rainy Daye. I wear many hats here, but mainly head the youth and adult choirs and assist with the Wednesday night bible study group. I just wanted to stop in to say hello."

Scott smiled, as he welcomed and held the door open for her, "Please come in, Rainy, and what's this?" he asked as he eyed the cake she was holding.

"Thanks, oh this is just a little something to welcome you to our church." She handed him the cake. *At last, a friendly face* thought Elea, as she turned and walked toward the door where Rainy stood.

Scott proceeded to introduce Rainy to Elea and to everyone, and welcomed her to sit. The volunteers then congregated around the room as Rainy told everyone a little bit about herself. She was in her early fifties, unmarried, living in her deceased parents' home a half a mile down the road, had attained a graduate degree from Centreville College of Music, and had taken on the role of youth and adult choir director. She was still in that role after fifteen years and loved her music ministry. Both choirs, she explained, met on Wednesday evenings, the same night as the weekly bible study. After a pleasant and informative conversation with Rainy, the volunteers disbanded and resumed their discussions with one another.

As Elea led Rainy to the door, she thanked her for the cake, and then asked, "Do you have a few minutes to chat, Rainy? It IS 'Rainy', correct? And your last name is 'Daye'?"

Rainy chuckled, "Yes, of course, and my unconventional name comes from the day I was born. It obviously was on a 'rainy day' when mom delivered me."

Elea smiled and chuckled, "I love it!" She continued, "Let's step outside. It's a gorgeous night tonight. I'll cut us pieces of that delicious-looking cake you brought over, and we'll have some coffee."

"Thanks," Rainy replied with a big smile. Both women took seats on the top step of the dorm and started to chat.

Elea proceeded to explain to the choir director what had transpired with regard to Kyle, the associate pastor, and his indifference toward her and Scott that first day in Reverend Ward's office. She also told Rainy what had happened that morning after services with Beth and her small group of women friends. Elea wondered if Rainy knew the reason why Kyle and Beth were on the abrasive side to her, and wondered why they were so against the assistance from their volunteers.

"Oh, I can tell you," said Rainy, "The associate pastor, Kyle Williams, is a widower. That was his seven-year old son, Jack, with him. He lost his lovely wife, Haley, three years ago in a fatal car crash. At the time, she was pregnant with their second child, a little daughter. He's still dealing with it. Since that time, Kyle's whole character and personality seemed to have changed. Ten years ago when he and his wife settled into the community, he was friendly, enthusiastic and loved his life here at the church. He was involved in all areas, helped so many people and was always busy accommodating and serving the entire church and community. Our congregation adored him. Intellectually, looks-wise and personality-wise, they loved him. Since the tragic time of losing both his wife and unborn baby girl, he pretty much keeps to himself and rarely interacts with the congregation anymore. He's mainly seen at Sunday services with Jack. He leaves it up to Everett to preach, but there was a time when he was filled with the spirit of God, which was clearly evident through his sermons. He's a smart guy who's been working on his Doctor of Theology degree. It's Everett's hope that Kyle will one day replace him as pastor once he retires. And that may be soon, as the Reverend is in his mid-eighties."

Rainy added, "I know he dates Beth Leiden, who's Everett's assistant. She's the church secretary, is divorced and has no children. She's had her eye on Kyle since the day she arrived, even when Haley was still alive. Even Haley was uncomfortable with Beth's presence, and how she would always conveniently position herself wherever Kyle was. Beth would always be in Kyle's face and would look for reasons to stop into his office. She convinced Everett to offer her the position of church assistant when Corrie Jackson retired, just so that she could be in close proximity to his office. I'd say Beth has been in this community for the past seven years. She lives in an apartment nearby. I know she would love to live with Kyle, but he's made no efforts to welcome her to do so. She's kept company with him for the past three years, following Haley's death. Beth is also the coordinator of the Wednesday evening bible study. She and Kyle ask me to child sit for Jack when they go out. To be honest with you, a lot of the congregation isn't fond of her. She's very rude and controlling. She and a few of the other women are friends with one another, and they all do what she says. I know she's influenced Kyle's way of thinking, and has Reverend Ward's ear most of the time. The more devout and elderly members of our congregation see right through her, yet her own clique of friends think she's the best thing that's happened to this church."

"Wow, you sure know these people very well, Rainy! So I guess that explains Kyle's personality, as well as Beth's. I'm very sorry for his loss. We'll work hard to change their minds about our outreach program and our purpose for being here," Elea replied.

Rainy and Elea exchanged a few more pleasantries, along with each other's cell phone numbers, and said they looked forward to working with and helping each other. Elea went back inside and picked up on her discussion with Scott regarding Kyle and Beth. She relayed to him what Rainy had told her. And she also expressed to Scott how she felt she made a new friend in this lovely woman, Rainy.

Judy S. Wagner

CHAPTER 3

ELEA MENTIONED TO SCOTT, "BEFORE I forget, I have to call Lane. I told him I would connect with him after I arrived to let him know the status of things here."

Scott asked, "So how's that relationship going with you guys?"

Elea replied, "Well, we've been dating since college, which is where we met. My being here and away from him for these next six months will be a test of our relationship. I'm hopeful, though, that when we connect by the holidays, he'll pop the question."

Lane Hudson was Elea's investment broker boyfriend with whom she was in a long-term relationship. He was handsome, successful and made a lucrative career for himself. Lane owned an elegant Metro Line City apartment, two expensive cars, and enjoyed the finer things in life. Elea, on the other hand, relinquished her affordable apartment when she first became active in the outreach ministry. Throughout occasional visits to Metro Line City, she would be the guest of her best friend, Selene Walker. Selene also maintained an affordable apartment in the heart of the city.

Lane and Elea made a beautiful couple. Both in their late-twenties, people often stared at them wherever they went. They had met in their freshmen years of college, became instantly attracted to each other, and immediately started to date. Elea majored in the social sciences, having attained her Masters in Social Work degree, and Lane majored in Business Administration. He took a number of courses in finance, accounting, statistics, economics, and quantitative analysis. His goal in life was to become financially independent and successful, a goal he attained within record time upon completion of his graduate degree from school. He was also employed by a reputable investment brokerage firm in Metro Line City.

Elea looked forward to talking to him. When she phoned, he didn't answer, so she left a voicemail message for him. She was excited when he phoned back the next morning as she was having breakfast with Scott and the volunteers.

"Lane said he's looking forward to when I make it back to New York during Christmas break. He said he's anxious to talk to me in person. This HAS to be it, Scott; I'll bet he'll propose!" Elea was over the moon, as that possibility appeared strong.

Early in the week, the outreach volunteers held meetings at separate times in the church's fellowship hall. They met with the adults, elderly members and a small teen ministry group that had just been formed, thanks to Rainy. The purpose was to discuss in full detail exactly what the needs were, and how to prioritize and plan out the work.

Elea, Scott, the volunteers, the teens, adults and elderly members shared fruitful discussions and humor at these meetings. Elea noticed how Kyle and Beth kept their distances as the meetings were taking place. She also noticed how Kyle and Beth looked at each other, smirked, and rolled their eyes whenever a church member asked to join the meeting. They both were obviously unhappy with this whole endeavor and were making their feelings abundantly clear.

The following day, Elea and half of the volunteers started working among the elderly congregation members, as Scott and the other half of the volunteers started working among the teens and adults.

"Knock-knock, Mrs. Ellison, I'm heading to the grocery store, what can I pick up for you?" Elea asked, as she poked her head through Mrs. Ellison's front door.

"Oh, thank you dear, come in, I have my grocery list all ready for you," replied Mrs. Ellison.

"Great, thanks, your's makes the last list for the store. The volunteers and I will now be heading to the store to do everyones' food shopping," Elea replied with a smile.

Two days a week were targeted for the elderly community's grocery shopping. For those who were able to get out, they were transported to Crenshaw's Groceries, located on the main country road. For those homebound and disabled members, Elea collected their lists, disseminated them among the volunteers, and everyone shopped for them.

Elea and some of the volunteers also house cleaned the homebound and disabled seniors' homes once a week. If any repairs needed to be made to their homes, Scott and other male volunteers, along with some assistance from the adult church members, tackled the work.

CHAPTER 4

A UGUST HAD PASSED, AND EARLY September arrived. The congregation was very happy with the Catholic volunteer workers. They were already making a significant difference in the lives of the elderly, teenagers, and other members within the small community. Elea and her volunteers were doing an amazing job working among the senior community with transportation to hair appointments, barber shops, medical visits, grocery shopping, reading and visitation time, housework and meal preps. The volunteers, teen ministry, and adult church members joined together with providing basic home repairs, yard work, painting, in addition to helping to make immediate repairs on the outside of the church. Once having completed a good deal of repair work, everyone who helped was treated to grilled food and ice cream. Sunday was always considered the "Day of Rest" with morning church services, followed by hospitality hour in the fellowship hall, and whenever possible, fun picnics in the local park.

Reverend Ward called a meeting after the first month with Scott, Elea and all of the volunteers. Everyone met in the fellowship hall. Kyle and Beth were also in attendance.

"It's my understanding there's a lot of good work being done around here," Reverend Ward proudly stated, as he smiled at the two coordinators, "Both of you and your volunteers are doing an excellent job for our church and community. We're very grateful to you. Everyone seems to be quite happy with the work you're doing."

Zoning in on Elea, Beth spoke, "Oh, I don't know, Mrs. Petersen didn't seem all that happy with the house cleaning two of your volunteers did for her. She said their work should've been inspected by YOU before they left her house."

Elea, caught off guard, apologized as she faced Beth, "I'm sorry, I'll speak to both Mrs. Petersen and to the women who cleaned for her."

Beth added as she faced Scott, "As far as the painting of Mr. Taylor's garage, he said it was an 'ok' job, but several spots were missed. That was something YOU needed to inspect."

Scott replied, "I'm also sorry, I'll speak to Mr. Taylor and to the two guys who helped paint his garage."

Beth added, "In the past three years, when Kyle and I ran things, we had just selected a few of our volunteers to work on those projects, and there were never any complaints." She stared at Elea with a look of condescension.

Elea tried to remain calm, yet was moved to frustration. She felt she needed to speak up, however with a diplomatic approach. "We're trying, Beth, our workers have a lot on their plates and no one's ever sitting down relaxing. We're trying to make a difference in this lovely community that needs a great deal of help. This is purely volunteer work, and we do need a little support." She added, "You and Kyle are welcome to also loan a helping hand to everyone, as we could certainly use YOUR help, as well."

Kyle zoned in on Elea and frowned. With coldness in his voice he responded, "We understand, but you people came to us, we didn't invite you here. This is YOUR initiative, and not OUR'S. Why should we be obliged to help when we don't feel the need for all of you to be here in the first place?"

Elea's mouth hung open. His awful remark hit home! She faced Scott and could feel angry emotions starting to surface. She replied, "Excuse me." And with that, she left the room disgusted. Scott also was disgusted. He frowned, shook his head, excused himself as well, and followed Elea, calling her name as he left the room. The volunteers all faced one another, obviously feeling uncomfortable and confused with the discussion that had just taken place. They, too, excused themselves and exited the meeting room, leaving Reverend Ward, Kyle and Beth alone by themselves.

Reverend Ward, clearly unhappy, sat back in his chair, glared at Kyle and Beth, then spoke, "I'm very much ashamed of the two of you. We're supposed to be a family of christians here. Those volunteers have arrived of their own free will for the purpose of assisting and serving our community in order to make a difference. At least make them feel welcome and appreciated. Now please get ahold of yourselves and exercise a little christian charity where they're concerned." He paused, then added, "And I agree with Miss Johnson that both of you should also help them."

He shook his head, closed the notebook he had brought with him, and didn't cast a backward glance at Beth and Kyle as he got up and left the fellowship hall disgusted.

Eager to "smooth things over" with the Reverend Ward, while also reflecting on his own role as the church's associate pastor, Kyle approached Scott and Elea the following day. He offered both his apologies and assistance to help the workers.

Beth, on the other hand, convinced Reverend Ward that she had a good deal of "church business" to tend to. And while not tending to those responsibilities, claimed that Kyle depended on her help with looking after his young son, Jack.

CHAPTER 5

S COTT AND ELEA WERE EXTREMELY successful with recruiting additional church volunteers who had suddenly "come alive" and were eager to assist with whatever work needed to be done.

For a bit of leisure time, Scott planned a family night walk. Being an outdoors person and fascinated by science, he noted to everyone the various insects and wildlife one usually doesn't see during the day. He had gotten ahold of reflective vests and headlamps so everyone would be able to be seen throughout the walk. Kyle, Beth and Jack attended the event. Elea and other volunteers joined the participants later that evening on the church grounds for an outdoor movie session. The women distributed blankets, pillows, and popcorn, while the men provided the movie and equipment needed.

The following week, the male volunteers took the youth members on a camp out. Everyone toted their sleeping bags and camped out under the stars. Fathers were also invited and encouraged to attend. Kyle accompanied Jack to the local campsite, as well. It was a great way for dads and their sons to reconnect to the natural world.

The next morning after Elea and the female volunteers distributed donuts, coffee and juice to the participants, Kyle thanked Scott as he was ready to leave with Jack.

Scott smiled and admitted, "I have to confess this wasn't my doing. You can thank Elea for the idea and for her help in pulling this all together; the woman's a great organizer."

Elea stood nearby, chatting with some of the parents and smiling at the participants as they were leaving. She was pleased the camp out had been such a great success.

Kyle, smiling, approached her with Jack. Elea faced him with surprise.

"Hi, I just wanted to thank you. Jack and I really enjoyed ourselves," Kyle said, as he glanced down at his son and put his hand on Jack's head.

He stood staring at her for a few seconds, his piercing light green eyes and gorgeous smile fixed directly on her. It was the first time she noticed he actually was capable of smiling. *What a well-built handsome man he is,* she thought.

She drifted for a minute, and then shook herself out of the mesmerizing moment. She replied, "Oh great, I'm so happy you both enjoyed yourselves!"

She bent down to talk to Jack, "We're going to need a little help with the Christmas pageant we hope to plan for December. Would you like to be in it?"

Jack shyly looked up at his dad, "How about it buddy?" Kyle asked, smiling down at his son. Jack nodded his head.

Elea replied, "Wonderful! I'll discuss that more in detail with you, probably by November," she smiled as she faced Kyle. He nodded, smiled, continued staring at her for a few more seconds, then took Jack by the hand and left.

"Come in, come in, Elea," welcomed Reverend Ward.

"Thanks, Reverend Ward; I'll just need a few minutes of your time to update you on how our fall agenda is being planned. In addition to our ongoing work projects, there will also be a series of activities which will certainly keep everyone busy and having fun."

Just then, Kyle knocked on the door and poked his head in. He noticed Elea was speaking with Reverend Ward.

"Oh, sorry for the interruption, I was just looking for Beth. I wanted to let her know our date is postponed for tonight because I can't find a sitter for Jack. I've been trying to contact Rainy, but there's been no answer for a couple of days now."

Reverend Ward responded, "I must be getting old and forgot to mention that Rainy is away for the month visiting with her sister in North Carolina."

Kyle looked disappointed, "Ok, thanks." He started to close the door.

Elea responded, "I might be able to help you with Jack tonight."

Kyle turned and faced her while still holding onto the door. "Really? Are you sure?"

Elea replied, "Yes, take Beth out and enjoy yourselves. Jack and I will get along fine together. I just need your address and I'll be there when you let me know the time." She observed the look of happiness on his face.

"Hey thanks, how about by 6:00 P.M.?" he asked.

"You got it," Elea confirmed.

"Everett has my address, I don't live far," he responded, as he smiled and faced her with a look of sincere gratitude.

Elea couldn't believe she was volunteering to help this man and his girlfriend who had been so rude to her! *Did I just offer to do something nice for him?* she asked herself, shaking her head.

Six o'clock arrived and Elea knocked on the door to Kyle's small, modest-looking country home. It was quite the change from the venue in New York to which she had been accustomed. The area was blissfully quiet, aside from the sounds of crickets, and fireflies flickered throughout the air. She didn't arrive empty handed. She brought over some children's books, a couple of hero adventure movies and a huge tub of three different varieties of popcorn. Scott loaned her a telescope, for in the event Jack was curious about the sky, and wanted to stargaze and explore the planets.

Kyle answered the door, smiling, and looking surprised, "Hi, what's all of this?"

"I just brought over some things Jack and I might have some fun with while you're on your date," Elea smiled as she stared into his handsome face.

Kyle shook his head and chuckled, "Okay, I'll let my little guy know you're here." He called for Jack. The shy little boy walked slowly up to his dad and stood.

"Hi sweetheart," Elea said, as she stooped down to face him, "I'm looking forward to spending some time with you tonight. I brought over books, two great hero adventure movies, some delicious popcorn and a telescope if you want to go outside later and check out the stars and planets." Jack looked up at Elea and smiled. It was the first time that she ever saw him smile.

"Okay then, I'll leave now and won't return too late. Jack, listen to Miss Elea and I'll be back to bring you upstairs and tuck you in a bit later. Love you, son."

Kyle smiled at Elea, "Thanks again for helping me; he should be fine for you."

Elea and Jack enjoyed a wonderful evening for the four hours they spent together. Jack couldn't wait to use the telescope, stargaze and explore the planets. Jack and Elea watched the two movies while munching on the tasty popcorn. She guided him afterwards into getting into his pajamas and brushing his teeth and then read to him. She covered both of them up with a super hero blanket, as he sat with his head leaned against her arm. He had started to fall asleep, so she grabbed a pillow and let him remain on the sofa covered with the blanket.

She got up, took a seat across the room, and attempted to dial Lane. Once again, no answer when she tried reaching him, even when she dialed his emergency cell phone number. She left her usual voicemail message. It was frustrating. Since her arrival in Tennessee, not once had he been available whenever she tried reaching out to him. As she was buried deep in thought, she heard the front door opening. Kyle had returned from his date with Beth. She motioned for him to quietly enter the room, as Jack was sound asleep on the sofa.

Kyle smiled at her as he quietly whispered, "How was he? Any problems?"

Elea smiled and replied, "Just adorable! He's such a sweet child. We had a great evening together. I got him into his pajamas for you and had him brush his teeth. He's all ready for you to bring him up and tuck him in."

Kyle was very pleased, "I can't thank you enough!" He reached for his wallet to pull out money.

"Oh no, I couldn't," Elea insisted, "You don't owe me anything. It was such a pleasure taking care of him. If you need me again, I can help."

Kyle grew serious as he stared into her eyes with a look she couldn't describe, caught himself in the awkward moment, and then diverted his attention to Jack.

"Well, thank you again," he replied.

"Goodnight," and with that said, Elea smiled and saw herself out.

The next morning, Kyle and Jack were having breakfast.

"I really liked Miss Elea, dad. We had a lot of fun. Can she come back again?"

Kyle faced his son with a surprised look. It was the first time he had heard Jack get excited over any sitter who had ever watched him, "So you really liked Miss Elea?"

"Uh huh," replied Jack, as he nodded his head, "I liked her a lot. Can you go out again tonight so she can come over to watch me?" he asked, as he enthusiastically ate his breakfast.

Kyle noticed how his son, prior to Elea's spending time with him, always seemed bored with his sitters. It was as if a sudden "breath of fresh air" had come along to excite Jack and enable him to smile again. He hadn't seen his son smile since before the tragedy with his wife, Haley.

"We had a great time together, Scott!" Elea told her fellow coordinator over breakfast, "That little Jack is so adorable. He's a sweet child. I also noticed how his good looks favor his dad's."

As she sipped her coffee, she suddenly became melancholy.

"What's up, Elea?" Scott asked her.

"I don't understand it. I tried phoning Lane last night. Apparently, the guy has gone AWOL on me again. I checked my cell phone messages, and still no word from him. Why would he be so anxious to talk to me when I head home at Christmas time? He didn't sound alarmed or anything, but I don't understand why he's either not returning my calls or calling at random," she replied.

"You don't suppose he's seeing other women, do you?" Scott asked with reservation, hoping that he hadn't crossed the line with her.

"I would hope not, Scott," Elea replied, then continued, "We love each other and have been together for a long time. If anything, our relationship should move forward, not backward." She tried to convince her own self of that, as she responded to him. That thought, however, DID cross her mind.

Scott shrugged and said, "Okay, let's get moving, lady, we have a lot to do today."

"Yes, we sure have," she replied.

Scott, Elea and their volunteers were hard at work continuing on with their mission of assisting the elderly and underprivileged members of the church and local community. Beth still maintained her usual rudeness toward Elea whenever they crossed paths. She was clearly unhappy after she had heard that Elea sat for Jack the evening she and Kyle were on a date. She was especially angry in learning how Jack looked forward to Elea sitting for him again in the future.

"Well, I'm afraid I have some bad news for the congregation of the Evangelical Community Church," said Reverend Ward, as he addressed the members at Sunday services that weekend. He continued, "I'm holding a letter from our choir director, Miss Rainy Daye. Miss Daye's elderly sister, Greta, with whom she's currently visiting in North Carolina, has taken ill and will need a good deal of home care. So Miss Daye has already made arrangements to reside at her sister's home for an indefinite period of time. She states she'll return to our church sometime in the future, but won't be immediately returning as our choir director."

Kyle then asked if he could address the congregation, "In Rainy's absence, I'll temporarily step in and will work with everyone. Those of you who have been choir members for years may need to guide me through this process." Reverend Ward seemed grateful and thanked him.

Kyle would have need for a sitter for Jack on a Wednesday evening, as there would be a conflict with Beth's bible study taking place the same night. Beth thought of that. She asked to speak to the congregation. Reverend Ward nodded to her.

"Associate pastor Kyle will have an ongoing need for a sitter for his son Jack on Wednesday evenings. Anyone who's interested, please let me know and you'll be interviewed. This person should be a volunteer from our teen ministry."

Having stated that, she faced Elea with a fiendish smirk on her face. Elea's heart sank and she looked disappointed. Kyle noticed the interaction between them and wasn't happy. He frowned at Beth from where he was seated on the altar.

After services, when everyone had traveled downstairs to the fellowship hall, he called her aside, "What was THAT all about, Beth? I'M the one in charge of my son's life and determines who looks after him. Besides, I don't necessarily prefer someone from our 'teen' ministry being responsible for Jack!"

Before Beth could respond, Jack approached them, "Dad, can I go sit with Miss Elea at her table for a donut and juice?"

Kyle nodded, "Sure, son."

Beth then stalked off, obviously unhappy with Kyle's response. She joined her clique of friends and whispered to them, while focusing on where Elea sat with Scott and all the volunteers.

A few minutes later, Kyle joined Elea, Jack, and everyone at their table. He asked Elea, "Will you be comfortable with looking after Jack on Wednesday evenings?"

Elea was surprised, as she was still numb over Beth's announcement to the congregation, and replied,

"I'll be happy to. There shouldn't be issues with helping on that night. Besides, he's such a sweetheart."

Kyle stated, "Well, I know he likes YOU a lot."

She privately asked Kyle, "If I ever had to keep him over at our facility, say, you won't return until the next day, would that be an option?"

"Yes, of course, but I don't anticipate being anywhere overnight at any time." Kyle focused downward, clearly understanding what Elea meant. Sensing her thoughts about Beth, he looked up at her and added, "It's not like that at all."

As he was finishing his juice, Jack asked, "Dad, can we take Miss Elea on a picnic with us sometime?"

"Sure, if Miss Elea isn't busy. But she and her friends have a lot of work here to do at our church. There are many projects lined up, and the weather's getting a little colder now with the season changing," Kyle explained to his son.

"Your dad's right, Jack. But you know, you and I will have Wednesday nights to look forward to," Elea reassured him.

Jack was thrilled and replied, "We do!" and with that, he put his arms around Elea's neck and tightly hugged her. She also held him tight as she closed her eyes. Kyle tenderly smiled as he gazed at them and thought, *What a special woman she is, and Jack really loves her.*

Members of the small community church soon observed the welcome, positive changes in their associate pastor, Kyle. He was now actively engaged and showed a bright and renewed interest in the church, as he had once shown prior to his wife's passing. Both Reverend Ward and the congregation were pleased. The senior board of deacons agreed it was due to the efforts of the outreach coordinators, and their volunteers. Thanks to their positive influence, their associate pastor was gradually returning to his calling to serving the Lord.

CHAPTER 6

L ATE SEPTEMBER AND THE FALL season arrived with its colorful foliage, harvest celebrations, pumpkin-spice lattes and apple cider. Various fundraisers were being held throughout the small community for projects such as church refurbishing, handicap ramps, floor and wall repairs, and indoor and outdoor painting. Those projects would be started, and then completed by the following spring season. The church itself was old and was in dire need of repairs. It was obvious the building had been neglected for many years.

Elea and the volunteers worked with the adults and elderly church members in the holding of bake sales in order to raise funds. They made and sold sweet potato pies with macaroon crust, cranberry-apple lattice pies, and bourbon pecan pies. Other varieties included pumpkin, coconut custard, orange-cranberry, mince and lemon meringue. They also sold multiple varieties of cookies, assorted muffins, caramel apple and granola crisps, and apple gingerbread cakes. Elea was pleased that the bake sales raised a good amount of funds toward painting the inside of the church, a priority item that was near and dear to the heart of Reverend Ward. Certain members of the teen ministry were football players and cheerleaders at the local high school and also helped raise funds for the church. The teen ministry hosted community car washes, cookie bake sales, and staged five-mile hikes through the parks among falling leaves.

Outside projects were in progress by the volunteers, in addition to assistance from available members of the adult community. Then on weekends, the teen ministry contributed time and work to assisting. Additional volunteers under the coordinators' guidance worked on projects for the elderly such as fence painting and outside repairs to their properties, lawn mowing, weed pulling, leaf raking, planting bulbs for the spring season, and other necessary maintenance work.

In addition to these work-related projects, the fall was also a fun season for visits to local farms on weekends. Scott and Elea scoped out nearby venues in the area for the purpose of planning a schedule of fun events for the church and community. One sixty-five acre property, Season Time Orchards, offered pony rides, wagon hayrides into pumpkin patches, a huge corn maze, scavenger hunts, and play tractors. There were eye-pleasing seasonal displays of colorful mums, pumpkins, hay bales and other festive fall decorations set up at the entrance to the farm.

Season Time Orchards also offered apple and pumpkin picking, apple cider donuts, wines, assorted pies and muffins and a small indoor market of fresh fruits and vegetables. The farm offered educational programs. They held story time about animals and farming equipment, crops, how apple trees grow and even pumpkin carving. On certain weekends, even local bands were scheduled for entertainment purposes.

A week before Halloween, the volunteers hosted a family event to visit Season Time Orchards for the day. Elea noticed that Kyle, Beth and Jack had all arrived together. As usual, Beth stared at Elea as she took hold of Kyle's arm. Beth, as always, made sure Elea noticed.

When everyone congregated at the farm's entrance, Scott proceeded to review the guidelines by which all visitors were asked to abide.

"This is especially important for when everyone enters the massive corn maze scheduled for late this afternoon. We're all to meet at the maze entrance by 4:00 p.m. From there, we'll take a headcount to ensure our entrance and exit numbers match up. This farm is huge, so everyone here should be accompanied by a 'buddy'".

Elea scanned the congregation and nodded in agreement with her fellow coordinator. The congregation disbanded and everyone, tickets in hands, dispersed to various areas of interest.

Jack left his father's side after speaking with him and made his way toward Elea, "Hi, Miss Elea, will you be my buddy when we get into the corn maze?" he asked as he pointed toward the direction of where the maze was located.

"Of course, honey, that is, if it's alright with your dad."

Jack proceeded to ask Kyle. He ran back to Elea looking happy, "He said it's fine."

Elea glanced over at Kyle who smiled and nodded his head. Elea reciprocated the smile, despite the dirty looks she was receiving from Beth.

All of the volunteers traveled with the congregation and assisted the elderly members with their wheelchairs, walkers, and bathroom necessities. They also kept them hydrated and provided sun hats to them for areas that became especially hot and humid. While the temperatures became cooler in the month of October, the sun managed to provide its warmth in certain areas. The teen ministry acted independently and went off in groups, some holding the hands of smaller children.

Elea wheeled widowed Mrs. Ellison around in her wheelchair. The elderly citizen and life-long member of the senior board of deacons, was enjoying the day. She was most appreciative to be comfortable as she admired nature's beauty and was fascinated by the gorgeous fall foliage. She laughed as a random colorful tree leaf dropped into her lap.

"Let's get you something to eat and drink, Mrs. Ellison," Elea suggested, as she smiled.

"You are such a dear, Elea! How I wish our handsome associate pastor was dating YOU instead of that other *woman!*" Elea, caught off guard, laughed and felt a bit put on the spot.

Mrs. Ellison continued, "Some of us old people here were chatting at our knitting meeting yesterday. We all agreed you would make a much better girlfriend for Kyle than that awful woman he goes with!"

Elea laughed, "I heard he's been going with her for a while now and they're in a relationship. At least that's how I understand it. His young son, Jack, is adorable, and I even got to sit for him. It's a shame about the tragedy of Kyle losing his wife and unborn child." Elea looked sad, and shook her head, "I guess we have no idea what God has in store for us. It's a shame, especially for Jack. When I first met him, he looked so lost."

"No one forgot that day, honey, especially when Kyle first received the news. It changed his life completely. I've been praying for the young man in the hopes he'll find love again and that his young son will have a new, loving step-mother in his life. I'm not at all pleased with the company he's currently keeping."

Mrs. Ellison had been focused in the direction of where Kyle and Beth stood smiling and admiring the horses.

Four o'clock arrived. The congregation members and all volunteers met at the entrance to the massive sixty-five acre farm's corn maze, with everyone surprisingly being right on time. Scott gathered everyone together and spoke to the adults.

"Okay, folks, this is our last attraction of the day. Once we make it out of the corn maze, everyone will make tracks toward the parking lot and head home. It's getting cooler now and will be darker in another hour. Make sure everyones' been to the restrooms, have on your jackets and sweaters, have water or a snack with you, make sure your cell phones have fully-charged batteries, and that you have your flashlights working. Some of you managed to secure maps of the maze, and we've distributed glow sticks to the youth members. Watch towers and corn crops. Stay focused on where you're going. Most importantly, while the maze is a lot of fun, it can also be a dangerous place if you get lost and can't manage your way out. So exercise with caution, please. Now let's check out our 'buddy system'. Who's all teaming up with whom? And groups of you boys will need to be accompanied by grown-ups."

Elea, looking very attractive in her fall sweater, jeans and boots, spotted Jack and motioned for him to join her. He smiled and ran over to her, "Are you all set, Jack? Let's us two buddies hang together in the corn maze." She smiled and took him by the hand, "Let me zip up your jacket, honey, as it's really getting chilly out here."

The church members and teens, in addition to Scott and the volunteers, Beth and Kyle, all headed into the maze and started to comfortably follow the crowd that had entered before them. Elea and Jack were last to enter. Elea needed first to tend to Mrs. Ellison who was getting cold. She needed to be wheeled over to a church member's car who opted not to stay for the corn maze event. This person would drive her home.

As Elea and Jack entered the maze, two of Jack's friends were further up ahead and nearly out of sight. He wanted to catch up to them, so he took it upon himself to let go of Elea's hand and started to run from her.

"Jack, remember you're not supposed to go through this maze without a buddy."

"I'll be fine, Miss Elea, I want to go with my friends," he said, as he glanced back at her and ran quickly to catch up to them.

Elea stepped up her walking, then started to run, but she couldn't catch up to Jack. She felt the color drain from her face. Up ahead in the maze was no sign of him. As Elea tried to make her way through the complicated maze, she realized she was alone. She looked up at the sky. Darkness was starting to settle in and it was becoming much colder. Her heart raced; nothing was making sense. She was clearly lost in the massive corn maze. Fear was setting in, as she thought of Jack and how she'd lost sight of him. Yet, he ran from her and there was no way she could've caught up with him. She started to pray.

Just then, in the near distant, she thought she heard a young child crying, "Jack, honey, is that you? Where are you?"

She heard his faint voice, "Over here, Miss Elea, I tripped and can't walk! I'm scared!"

Elea, hoping she took the right turn, flicked on her flashlight and managed through the darkness of the cornfield, only to spot Jack on the ground, holding onto his ankle and sobbing. He had apparently tripped over a corn stump and had fallen.

Elea knelt down and hugged him tightly, "Oh sweetheart, I'm just so glad I found you!"

Jack apologized, "I'm sorry, Miss Elea, that I ran off and didn't listen to you!"

She reassured him, "That's okay. The main thing is that I found you and that we're together. Let me call Scott's cell phone and let him know we pretty much can't find our way out of here. Imagine, you and I are lost in this corn maze together!"

To relieve tensions, she laughed and made light of the situation as she smiled and hugged Jack, though in reality, she was terrified. Jack snuggled closer to her, comforted by her protective arms around him. Scott was very relieved to get Elea's call.

"Elea, thank God! Where are you and little Jack? Kyle's over here with me and he's been very worried about his son!"

An hour had passed, and the church members had already left the farm to head back home. The only remaining visitors were Kyle, Beth, Scott, the owner of the farm, and some of his workers. It was totally dark outside at that point. Elea had powered up her flashlight, so she kept it on as she and Jack huddled next to each other on the ground.

"There they are!" She soon heard the voices of the farmer and the workers he had recruited to comb through the maze.

When Kyle saw Elea and Jack, he quickly picked up his son, hugged him tight and kissed him, while Beth looked on.

"Daddy, my ankle hurts, and I can't walk," Jack sobbed.

Elea explained, "Kyle, it looks like Jack tripped over a random corn stump."

Kyle glared at her and asked, "And where were you? Why was he not with you? I trusted you to watch my son in that maze!"

Elea responded, "If you'll just give me a minute to explain what happened … ."

Kyle frowned and shot Elea a look of disdain. He clearly didn't want to know anything, other than his son needing attention.

"Come on, Jack, Beth, let's go home," he said in a disgusted tone of voice.

Beth made sure she turned and smiled brightly at Elea, who was standing there feeling hurt and looking like she was on the brink of tears. Scott put a loving arm of support around her.

On the car ride home, Beth emphasized to Kyle that she felt Elea was much too irresponsible to help with Jack on Wednesday evenings. She did her best to try to convince him. Kyle just stared straight ahead as he drove home, but said nothing.

The next morning as Kyle and Jack were having breakfast before he took his young son to school, Jack said, "Daddy, I heard you and Miss Beth talking about Miss Elea last night. You both sounded like you don't like her very much. But I have something to tell you."

Kyle looked with surprise into the face of his son, "What's that, son?"

Jack explained, "It wasn't Miss Elea's fault that we got lost in the maze. We held hands going in, and then I stopped holding her hand and ran off with my friends. She kept calling my name, telling me to stop and stay where I was because I would get lost, but I didn't listen to her. I kept running until I didn't hear her voice anymore. I didn't see any of my friends up ahead, and then I tripped and fell. I couldn't get up. It got dark out and I heard Miss Elea calling my name. I tried to tell her where I was. She found me and said she would stay with me and would call someone to help us. She wasn't even mad at me. She just kept asking if I was okay and promised that she would never leave me alone in there. So, please don't be mad at her. It was MY fault for not listening to her."

Kyle breathed a huge sigh of relief, "Thank you for being honest with me, son. I believe I owe Miss Elea an apology."

Kyle looked serious and realized he made a mistake. He needed to apologize to Elea as soon as possible.

He phoned the dorm and Scott answered. "Hi, Scott, can you ask Elea to come to my office, please?"

Scott responded, "Sorry, Kyle, she's out food shopping for the seniors, but I'll tell her that you called."

Kyle responded, "Thanks, and can you tell her I'd really like to see her as soon as possible when she returns?"

It was hours later as Kyle still sat in his office, deep in thought. Elea had not acknowledged his message, nor arrived at his office. By day's end, he sent Beth over to his house to stay with Jack until he returned. He locked the church office door to drive into town. He purchased a large bouquet of beautiful fall flowers, and then made his way over to the dorm. He hoped he could speak to Elea and apologize for his harsh words to her from the previous night.

Scott answered the door and immediately focused on the flower bouquet. "Hi, Kyle, come in."

Kyle responded as he glanced around the room, "Thanks, is Elea here?"

At that moment, Elea happened to come into view as she was passing through with grocery bags. She spotted him, paused, put her head down, put the groceries on the countertop, and started taking everything out to sort them.

"Elea, can I talk to you?" Kyle asked, as he started to walk toward her. She paused from what she was doing, didn't look up, then turned her back toward him.

"Sorry, I'm busy," she responded. And with that, she continued her work sorting out all of the groceries.

Kyle sighed, placed the flower bouquet down, leaned his back against the countertop, folded his arms, and continued to speak.

"Elea, I'm really sorry about how I spoke to you yesterday. I spoke before I thought, and it was wrong of me to have overreacted the way I did. Jack let me know this morning what happened, and how his getting lost in that maze was due to him disobeying you. It certainly wasn't your fault. What can I say? I'm a jerk, can you please forgive me?"

He turned her around to face him, but she didn't speak or look up. He handed her the flower bouquet and hugged her. As he pulled her closer to him, he whispered in her ear, "Elea, please forgive me."

Wrapped in his warm embrace, she asked, "How's Jack's ankle?"

Kyle responded, his smiling face staring into her's, "He's fine, and it was nothing."

At that moment, his cell phone rang. Beth was calling. "Alright, I'll be there in a minute," he said, as he gave Elea another hug, said goodbye, and then left the dorm.

How about that? Scott thought, as he had witnessed everything. He especially noticed how Elea stood silently by the door once Kyle departed, thoughtfully gazing down at the gorgeous flower bouquet he'd given her as a means of apologizing.

Scott clearly recognized there was "a moment" shared between Kyle and Elea. He just shook his head and smiled.

Judy S. Wagner

CHAPTER 7

ON HALLOWEEN NIGHT, THE TEEN ministry members of the church hosted their own party. Everyone was invited. Hand-made candy corn invitations were distributed to the congregation in early October, so everyone could mark their calendars. Costumes were optional, but not mandatory, for the adults. The outreach volunteers didn't dress in them, as they were in attendance only to lend assistance to the teen ministry. It was mainly the younger children who wore the costumes.

Though the volunteers offered to assist the teen ministry, they insisted on running the event themselves. They even recruited a local DJ for music. The DJ charged very minimally for his services, as this was a church event. The outside of fellowship hall was graced with mums, pumpkins, scarecrows, spider webs and other festive inexpensive dime store Halloween decorations. The teens planned games and activities. Small prizes were going to be presented for the best homemade, cutest, scariest, funniest and most authentic costumes, for the most creative pumpkin designs, and for a dance contest for the adults.

The teen ministry even did an amazing job decorating the inside of the church's all-purpose fellowship hall. It was decorated with skeleton lights, festive paper pumpkin balls, a few ghost piñatas, bright-eyed cat garland, and reusable lanterns made out of old tins and pumpkin vases. In the back of the room was a pumpkin balloon backdrop, which would make a fun photo booth for everyone in costumes wishing to pose following the festivities. Tables of ten were arranged with black, orange and green inexpensive plastic tablecloths. There were spider web paper placemats, spider web designs on colorful paper napkins, and stick centerpieces made of regular branches sprayed green and placed in vases. Small baskets of Halloween snack mix were also put on each table, consisting of chocolate covered pumpkin pretzels, cheese crackers, and chips. Cold sandwiches from a local deli were ordered, and dessert contributions were requested from whoever was able to bake. There were cupcakes, cheesecakes, and the usual selection of homemade pies and cookies. Drinks included a punch bowl filled with pomegranate juice, seltzer and an icy hand frozen in a latex glove. There was "witches brew" in a clear punch bowl, filled with lemon-lime seltzer and lime sherbet. Water and varieties of cold sodas were also available, in addition to the regular apple cider. A coffee and tea station was set up in the back of the room.

Elea, Scott and the volunteers insisted on contributing toward the party. They paid for the cost of the DJ, the deli sandwiches, and reimbursed the teen ministry for the cost of the dime store decorations.

The congregation started to enter the room and the festivities were ready to begin. Kyle and Beth walked in with Jack.

As Elea and Scott stood drinking apple cider, Jack ran over to Elea. He was dressed as "Super Hero Man" and looked excited and adorable.

"Hey Jack, I really love your costume," smiled Elea, as she stooped down to face him. Jack smiled and was very flattered by Elea's response.

She stood back up and noticed how Kyle was smiling at her. He was smiling; Beth was shooting her dirty looks.

"Have fun, honey," Elea added, as Jack proceeded to leave her and run to his dad.

The teen ministry worked with the DJ they hired to announce the events. Reverend Ward sat at his table with Kyle, Beth, and some of the church's senior deacons. Throughout the evening, everyone was enjoying themselves, especially the children. The food, drinks and desserts were delicious, and the costume prizes had all been distributed. Judging those costumes were representatives from the senior board of deacons, Reverend Ward, and even Scott, who was very flattered to have been asked.

The last event of the evening was the adult dance contest. The teen ministry alone was going to judge that event. Elea loved to dance, but beforehand remarked to Scott that she refused to be a part of that contest. Upon his insistence, she reluctantly entered herself into the event, hoping she wouldn't even be considered. Beth and her clique of women friends entered the contest, as well.

The music stopped, as Elea advanced on the dance floor. She was met by stares and looks of disdain from Beth and her friends. All who remained on the floor were Beth, one of her friends, and Elea. The DJ was going to play one final song before a winner would be selected.

"Well, look who thinks she can dance! I'm surprised you're still in this contest. You know this event wasn't meant to include YOU, it's just for us church members," Beth sarcastically remarked.

Elea ignored the remark and stood waiting for the music to begin. Beth and her friend made sure they stared Elea down with intimidating looks. While Elea felt uncomfortable, she was determined not to let Beth's and her friend's negative attitudes affect her dancing. No one told her, aside from Beth, that she wasn't welcome to be a part of the contest. The teen ministry was ready to eliminate one dancer after another, and the winner would remain until the end of the song. Throughout fellowship hall, all eyes were focused on the dancers.

Elea took a breath and lost herself in the music, reflecting back on her college party days where she and her friends danced in the clubs. She felt very comfortable moving to the song that was being played. Before she realized it, she, alone was still dancing as the song was ending. She clearly won the contest.

As she glanced around the room in unexpected surprise, Reverend Ward and Scott were standing up clapping, which motivated everyone else to do likewise. For a brief moment, she felt like a star.

"Elea Johnson is our winner!" happily announced the DJ. The prize was a small amount of donated money, which Elea promptly walked over and handed to Reverend Ward.

"Please use this small donation, Reverend, to put toward the church's spring repair work."

Reverend Ward was grateful, initially refused to take the money, but accepted it upon Elea's insistence.

It was the end of the evening. The congregation filtered out of the fellowship hall, including Beth who had stepped outside with her clique of women friends. There they stood gossiping about Elea winning the dance contest.

"Miss Elea, could you please pose with daddy and me in front of that thing?" asked Jack, as he pointed to the pumpkin balloon backdrop. Families had already started to form lines and pose for pictures. One of the teens had a camera and was taking photos of all of the families with their excited children in Halloween costumes.

"Sure, Jack," Elea responded, as Kyle was approaching them.

"Daddy, can you, me, and Miss Elea get our picture taken in front of that balloon thing over there?" he asked.

Kyle responded, "Well, if Miss Elea's okay with it, it's fine with me."

When it was their turn in line, the teen photographer instructed, "Okay, guys, Jack, please sit between your dad and Miss Elea." She zoned in on Kyle and Elea, "Can you two guys huddle in more together so you look like a family," she asked, without a second thought.

Elea awkwardly faced Kyle, "I'm sorry, I guess she didn't realize…"

"It's okay, we're good," responded Kyle, who smiled and complied with the request. His head and Elea's were touching as they hovered over Jack. The teen took the photo, and then they got up to allow the next family in line to pose in similar fashion.

"By the way, you're some dancer!" Kyle smiled, as he gazed at Elea.

"Something I love to do," she responded, smiling and returning his gaze.

"Ready to go home now, guys?" Beth asked, as she returned to the room, grabbed hold of Kyle's arm, and took Jack by the hand.

"Uh yeah, I guess we should leave now," responded Kyle, as he shook himself out of staring at Elea.

As they proceeded to walk out the door, Beth turned and frowned at Elea. *Yeah, goodnight to you, too, Beth*, Elea thought, as she stood there shaking her head.

She then proceeded to work with Scott and the volunteers to assist the teen ministry with their clean-up efforts of the all-purpose fellowship room, then congratulated everyone on a well-organized, fun event.

Judy S. Wagner

CHAPTER 8

NOVEMBER ARRIVED AND THE BEAUTIFUL season continued with its cooler temperatures, beautiful fall foliage, harvest celebrations, hayrides, pumpkin-spice lattes, caramel apples, s'mores and the smell of smoking fire pits. Folks usually dressed in warm, bulky sweaters and carried blankets to sporting events. They enjoyed everything the glorious, colorful season had to offer.

Thanksgiving Day was the main calendar holiday for that month. The outreach volunteers, dedicated church members and the teen ministry, had been hard at work organizing clothing drives. They were also collecting non-perishable donations for the local soup kitchen, and meeting to discuss ideas for a church Thanksgiving Day dinner. This dinner would take place in the fellowship hall for families who had no relatives living nearby, and who would be spending the holiday alone.

Elea suggested that a "Thank you, Lord" poster be placed on a wall in the church's entry foyer for the month of November leading up to Thanksgiving Day. Church members of all ages would be encouraged to use the black marker provided to express their thanks to God for individual blessings received. Everyone loved the idea. The large plain white poster was placed on the entry foyer wall in the church for all to write what was in their hearts. The congregation took full advantage of the poster and the members expressed their thanks.

On a refreshment break during one of the volunteer meetings, Elea stepped upstairs to chart the progress of the poster.

She noticed one "thank you" expression that was written with bright blue marker, instead of the standard black one. The expression read, "From Beth Leiden: Thank you, Lord, for Kyle and Jack, and for all the love Kyle and I share."

Elea's felt the color drain from her face. Moments later, she stepped back downstairs and joined Scott and the Thanksgiving Day committee.

"Scott, when the meeting's over, you need to see one of the writings on the 'Thank you, Lord' poster. I can't believe how Beth keeps on instigating and rubbing it in my face about her relationship with Kyle! And the crazy thing is that she doesn't even need to do that. In another month, I'll be headed back to the city to connect with Lane." Elea shook her head, as Scott did same.

The meeting ended, and Scott followed Elea to the upstairs foyer where the poster hung on the wall. He read the message.

"Well, my friend, you should know by now she's insecure with you being here," Scott replied as he shrugged and stared at Beth's message.

"What does that mean, that I should leave?" Elea asked, as she faced him with a serious look on her face.

"Not at all, Elea, it's HER problem. SHE needs to get over herself," Scott replied, as he patted his fellow coordinator on the back.

The evening before Thanksgiving Day, the adult members, teen ministry and outreach volunteers were hard at work organizing and bagging clothes for a local homeless shelter. They were accepting soup kitchen and food bank donations, baked goods, and donated turkeys. Early the next morning, the volunteers would head out to make their drop-offs to nearby communities who were most in need of food and clothing.

Thanksgiving Day arrived. Once again, the teen ministry enthusiastically assisted the outreach volunteers to ensure a wonderful day of thanks. The fellowship hall looked festive with fall wreaths, pumpkin and gourd displays, and acorn garlands. Rows of long tables were covered with plastic tablecloths. Smaller covered tables were arranged for the paper plates, utensils, cups and napkins. There was a separate table for main food contributions from the congregation, and another table for pies and other desserts. The room was tastefully decorated and smelled wonderful! One volunteer had secured a large-screen TV which was displayed, so football games could be watched.

"Welcome, Reverend Ward and Happy Thanksgiving!" Elea smiled, as she led the elderly pastor over to a table, "We would love it if you would sit with us."

Reverend Ward was very pleased, as he gladly took hold of Elea's arm and allowed her to escort him to the table. Scott afterwards joined them. He had just returned after having traveled out with a few of the volunteers who provided rides to the elderly members for this celebration.

Reverend Ward spoke, "Well, I see you, your volunteers and even members of our own congregation once again did a magnificent job! I hope you're not planning on leaving us anytime soon. From how I see things going, you can stay indefinitely, if you wish. I know the congregation has never been so happy and incredibly thankful for all of you!"

Scott responded, "Thank you for your support, Reverend Ward." He added, "Our agreement states we're here to serve your church and this community for six months, which time ends in February. Then it will be up to you if you would like to extend us for an additional six months. As a note of interest, Father Bud, who heads our outreach volunteer ministry, emailed me just the other day. Father stated that we could assist for a maximum time of eighteen months, should you need us."

Reverend Ward responded, "This is wonderful news! First thing tomorrow, I'll contact your priest and update him on your progress. I know our church's senior board of deacons will definitely agree to grant you all a six-month extension. In fact, they're already expressing how they'll really miss you when you all need to leave."

Elea knew Mrs. Ellison was one of the senior deacons who helped govern the small church for years. She also knew how much Mrs. Ellison felt blessed by the volunteers and all they were accomplishing. Scott was thrilled and thanked Reverend Ward.

However, Elea had reservations and forced a smile as she quietly responded, "Thank you, Reverend Ward."

"Let's discuss, Scott," Elea whispered to him, as she excused herself and asked to speak a moment to him. She shared her thoughts, "Scott, that means more of Beth's abuse. For no other reason, I would love to stay, but this is going to be stressful. The woman's always in my face about Kyle."

Beth, Jack and Kyle weren't in attendance at the church's Thanksgiving Day dinner that afternoon. Reverend Ward explained that Beth was going to cook a turkey for Kyle, Jack and herself. Elea was relieved knowing she would be spared verbal abuse from Beth, and would be able to enjoy herself socializing with friendly members of the congregation.

The Thanksgiving Day feast proved to be successful. All leftover food and desserts were collected and distributed to the homeless shelters for those less fortunate people in the local community.

Within a week, the teen ministry had posted Halloween and Thanksgiving Day pictures. They were posted in the upstairs foyer on the adjacent wall where the "Thank you, Lord" poster was displayed.

CHAPTER 9

S COTT AND ELEA HAD PREVIOUSLY discussed with their volunteers that they should plan some kind of a Christmas pageant. The pageant was suggested in order to prepare for the joyous birth of the Lord, and to welcome in the holiday season.

"Wow, we really are busy. Seems like we go from one occasion right into the next!" Scott exclaimed, "And this is in addition to everything else we're helping this church and community with!"

Elea suggested, "Maybe we should keep this Christmas pageant simple, Scott. We have enough adult members to help paint scenery, and a lot of the women here can sew really well. We'll buy the materials, keeping within our budget, of course, and select all of our characters from among the young ones. Their parents will be so proud of them once they see their children act out roles in this play, and the children will feel like stars. Let's announce a meeting in the coming week."

Right after Thanksgiving, the volunteers met with the teen ministry and adult congregation to secure ideas as to how to plan and stage a small Christmas pageant. They would need a script, a construction of a nativity scene, someone to liaise with Kyle on the choirs' song selections, securing of materials to assemble and paint, women and some of the elderly members to sew simple costumes, a narrator, the setting up of the performance areas, lighting, and someone to manage a cast party afterwards. Characters would need to be selected. The baby Jesus would be a doll with a blanket wrapped around it to be placed in a manger.

The evening the meeting was called, almost everyone in the congregation filled the fellowship hall, with every person eager and willing to help. Also in attendance were Kyle, Beth and Jack.

Scott coordinated the meeting, and Elea spoke to the congregation, emphasizing that December was a very busy month. She explained that the volunteer organization would be funding the pageant, and that costs would be kept to a minimum.

"The children will take on the roles in this pageant, and the teen ministry and adult members, including us volunteers, will be responsible for the painting, props, lighting, selection of Christmas carols, and costume creations. We would need someone to narrate the story, as well. It will be easy for our children, as there will be no speaking involved. The children will just act out the parts."

Everyone in the fellowship hall nodded their heads and smiled as Elea ended her presentation. As always, when she sat down and happened to glance over at

Beth, she was given the usual dirty looks. *I promised Jack a role in this pageant and am asking him to play the role of Joseph, no matter if SHE likes it or not,* Elea thought. She was growing tired of Beth's indifference.

The meeting ended, but all of the younger children with their parents were asked to remain. As Kyle, Beth and Jack were still sitting in their seats, Elea called, "Jack, can I talk to you?"

Kyle turned to face Elea, and then said to Jack, "Please go see what Miss Elea wants, she's calling you."

Jack walked over to Elea, who said, "Sit with me a minute, Jack, I would like to ask you something. How would you like to play the part of Joseph? He's one of the main characters in this nativity story."

Jack smiled as he faced Elea and nodded, "I would really like to do that, Miss Elea," he replied.

She responded, "Great, honey, please go ask your dad if it's alright. I just want to be sure."

Jack quickly ran over to Kyle who listened to what his son had to say. Kyle then glanced over at Elea, smiled and nodded. Beth rolled her eyes, and the three of them proceeded to exit the room.

As Elea scanned the remaining children in the hall, she spotted an adorable little girl, around the same age as Jack, and approached her.

"Hello, honey, to me you look like you would make a beautiful Mary in this play." The little girl shyly smiled and nodded her head. Elea added, "Where's your mom, we'll see if she'll let you play that part."

She heard a woman's voice behind her, "Excuse me?" Elea turned around. It was one of Beth's women friends.

Elea sighed, took the high road, and responded, "Hi, your little girl is adorable. In looking at her, I told her I thought she would make a beautiful Mary, the Mother of Jesus. Does she have your permission to play the part in this story?" Elea held her breath, as the woman hadn't made an effort to smile the entire time she was speaking to her.

Miraculously, the woman broke into a huge smile and responded, "Yes, that would be so wonderful! Oh, I'm Avalene, and my daughter is Ariana," and saying that, she extended her hand to Elea.

Elea was relieved, reached out to shake her hand, and smiled. She replied, "Oh, I'm so glad. Avalene, I'll need for you to stop in at our building tomorrow night to discuss Ariana's costume for the pageant."

Avalene responded, "Sure, just let me know how I can help you, Elea." And she excitedly took her daughter by the hand and exited the room.

Oh gosh, did she just call me by my name? Elea stood shocked and shook her head in disbelief. Avalene was one of Beth's women friends, but she certainly wasn't a snob once she and Elea actually met and spoke.

That evening, the remaining roles were requested of the various children who remained in fellowship hall with their parents. There were roles for everyone — shepherds, the inn keeper, the angels, and the wise men. Children were even willing to dress up as sheep, camels and horses. Everyone was happy and cooperative. Elea had volunteered to narrate the play, as none of the parents felt comfortable with speaking. Everyone agreed to help with everything that needed to be done, including with the rehearsals and working behind the scenes. In Rainy's absence, she and Scott spoke with Kyle regarding the youth and adult choirs' song selections for the play.

The small, informal, low-budget Christmas pageant took place on the third Sunday in December. The children all did so well! Elea was very proud of them. They all caught on as to what was expected of them throughout the few rehearsals that were held. Jack and Ariana both looked precious and heartwarming in their lead roles of Joseph and Mary. Kyle was beaming as Jack performed the role of Joseph in a most perfect way.

The cast party followed the pageant. Elea heard someone calling her name as she was headed over to the refreshment table for some water. She turned around. It was Kyle. "Elea, I just wanted to thank you so much again for asking Jack to play the part of Joseph. I can't tell you how thrilled he was since when you first asked him to do it. I've never seen him so happy!" And with that said, Kyle gave Elea a warm hug. Beth took note. At that moment, Reverend Ward got Kyle's attention. He released Elea and proceeded to walk over to the pastor.

Beth strolled over to where Elea stood. With an attitude, she faced her and said, "Excuse me, I took this poster down from the entry foyer wall. Thanksgiving's over, and I was waiting for 'you' people to take down your 'decorations' so Christmas news can be posted. Here's your 'Thank you, Lord' poster. I was wondering if you read everyones' messages."

Elea knew exactly what she meant, "Uh no, I haven't had the time to read what everyone's written," she replied, stating an obvious white lie. She just didn't want to give Beth the satisfaction, though she was upset when she first read the message.

"Well, you can have this back. And I would suggest you read ALL of the messages when you 'have time'".

Beth turned her back on Elea, then turned again to face her, "Oh, and I thought you should know I discovered THIS! It was displayed on the social events bulletin board." She tossed a picture which fell to the floor in front of Elea. Beth shot her a dirty look and walked away in disgust.

Elea bent down to pick up the photo. The picture Beth had tossed to her was the one of Kyle, Jack and Elea taken at the church's Halloween party. The three of them were posing in front of the pumpkin balloon backdrop and looking like a real family. All three of them looked wonderful in the picture. Obviously, Beth wasn't too thrilled at having stumbled across that photo which was displayed on the church's social events bulletin board. In studying it, she thought they clearly "looked" like a family. She refused to have it remain with the other family photos that were taken at the Halloween party.

Scott was in close proximity and happened to watch the interaction between the two women. He patted Elea on the back and said, "Here, let me have that poster and the picture, if you want. I know Reverend Ward would be interested in reviewing what his church members were grateful for on Thanksgiving Day, and I'm sure he'll appreciate this really great picture of you, Kyle and Jack."

Elea smiled as she stared at the picture, sadly shook her head, then handed it to Scott to give to Reverend Ward, along with the "Thank you, Lord" poster.

A few nights later, there was a knock on the door of the dorm. Scott answered it. There stood the group of teen ministry members. "Hi, could we talk to you guys?"

"Sure can," Scott replied, "What can we do for you?"

One of the teens replied, "We were thinking of planning a small Christmas dessert party one night during Christmas week, but prior to Christmas Day. We would put up a few decorations in fellowship hall, but wondered if you guys could help us. This would just be to wish everyone a Merry Christmas," explained one of them.

"Sure, come on in," Scott replied, as he welcomed the group of teens who were standing outside the door, shivering.

Elea took note and also welcomed them, "Hi, come in, could you guys go for some hot cocoa? It's so cold out there. We also have leftover cookies that're still fresh from the pageant a few days ago."

The group of teens was very grateful. They, along with Scott, Elea and the rest of the volunteers, helped decide on punch, tea, coffee, and baked goods for this informal gathering. Since funds would continue to come from the universal Catholic Volunteer Workers budget, there was no issue with shopping for the necessary items with which to host a small party. Inexpensive fir trees, lights, wreaths, and festive decorations were also purchased. Scott and Elea constantly worked to keep costs to a minimum.

The teen ministry also took the time after school to coordinate a Christmas toy drive for poor families of other neighboring communities, in addition to their own church's children's needs.

Christmas week arrived. Unfortunately, Elea had spent a little more time helping everyone to the point of exhaustion. She awoke at the crack of dawn the morning of the social. She helped the teen ministry with their toy distribution to all of the underprivileged families, along with the distribution of boxes of food and other necessary staples. She didn't attend the Christmas social that night because she was exhausted. She relaxed in the dorm and retired early that evening. She could hardly stay awake.

Over breakfast and coffee the following morning, two of the women volunteers informed Elea that Kyle had asked Scott where she was last night. He had been looking for her at the social. When Scott explained to him that Elea wouldn't be attending due to not feeling well, Scott noted that Beth seemed very happy.

The two women volunteers said that at the social, Beth made sure she was continuously vying for Kyle's attention. They explained how she even started to make inappropriate advances toward him. Kyle, embarrassed, tried to maintain his composure. He tolerated only so much of Beth's bad behavior, then proceeded to leave early with Jack that evening. Feeling ignored, Beth hung with her clique of friends for the remainder of the night.

Judy S. Wagner

CHAPTER 10

C HRISTMAS DAY ARRIVED. ALL OF the volunteers enjoyed a quiet day inside the dorm. They made calls to their families from up north to wish them a Merry Christmas, exchanged small presents, then they all ate dinner together. Everyone had contributed toward the decorating of the inside common area of the building. It looked bright and cheery with a fresh, huge evergreen tree decorated with multi-color lights, garland, and cute dime-store ornaments. Clear three-prong lights on plastic bases decorated the insides of the windows. The dorm looked like a happy and festive place for the holidays.

Elea remembered she had a gift for Jack and wanted to make sure he received it. She wouldn't be returning from Metro Line City until the second week in January to allow herself time to connect with Lane. She and Lane hadn't seen each other for months, and she looked forward to spending time with him. She didn't think it was necessary to mention to Kyle that she would be away. The youth and adult choirs, and the bible study, weren't scheduled to resume on Wednesday evenings until that second week in January. Elea would return before Wednesday and still be able to child sit for Jack. The volunteers and teen ministry were also taking a holiday reprieve from their ongoing projects.

Kyle spent Christmas Day with Beth, drove her home, then put Jack to bed. Elea softly knocked on the door later that evening and asked him if she could leave a gift for Jack. He seemed both surprised and happy to see her, insisted she come in, and offered her a glass of wine. He thanked her for the gift for his son and welcomed her to sit with him on the sofa.

They sat and chatted a while about Jack. They also discussed Kyle's role as a single parent with its many joys and challenges. Kyle, having grown more comfortable with Elea, eventually confided to her the personal tragedy he had experienced, and how he was still dealing with it. He explained at length to Elea how he had lost his wife, Haley, three years ago in a fatal car crash. And at the time, she was pregnant with their second child, a little daughter. He was also aware of the change in himself. Since that time of tragedy, he pretty much backed away from his involvement with the Lord and with his life at the church. Up until then, he explained how he was always involved and busy accommodating the church and entire community. He claimed he just wasn't ready to return to preaching, yet he acknowledged a time when he strongly felt the spirit of God within himself. It was evident in how he preached. He sadly reminisced the time of life when he, his wife and Jack were a happy family, and how thrilled he was when Haley told him she was pregnant with their second child.

Elea listened intently to Kyle's heartbreaking story. She felt his pain and couldn't emphasize enough how sorry she was over the loss of his cherished wife and unborn daughter.

Elea said, "I'll pray for you and Jack, Kyle, that one day God will send an angel into your lives."

He looked down as he sadly nodded and said, "Thanks."

They sipped their glasses of wine and discussed other topics, such as their family backgrounds and educations. Kyle explained that he's been working on his Doctor of Theology degree. He confided to her that Reverend Ward's wishes are that he will eventually replace him as the pastor of the church. The widowed, elderly pastor was coming very close to retirement. The board of senior deacons would first have to confirm Kyle's appointment, which would inevitably happen.

Elea responded, "I think you would make a wonderful pastor, Kyle! This church really needs an intelligent, strong leader to guide them."

Kyle again responded, "Thanks" in a modest fashion, as he faced downward and continued to sip his wine.

He asked Elea how she felt about her outreach ministry and working with the people of Scarlet Oak Valley.

She responded, "This is the best job I've ever loved! I've gotten to know so many wonderful people and families just in the short time I've been working with everyone. This is time that's been so meaningful and well spent. It's been such a very gratifying experience." He took note of her sincerity, beautiful smile, and the look of radiance on her face as she spoke.

Kyle stared at her in total fascination, put his wine aside, moved closer to her on the sofa, and pulled her in closer to him. He focused on her lips, and was about ready to kiss her.

Suddenly to Elea, this was becoming very real. At that point, she couldn't trust herself as to what would happen next. In haste she got up from the sofa, put her glass of wine down, grabbed her coat, excused herself and told Kyle she'd better be heading back to the dorm, as it was getting late.

As they both stepped outside onto the porch, he approached her from behind, put his arms around her waist, and turned her around to face him, "You are so beautiful," he said as he pulled her tightly into his arms and passionately kissed her. His lips were pressed firmly against her's and both of them were lost in a warm and loving embrace.

Caught up in that vulnerable moment, the reality of her relationship with Lane suddenly kicked in. She attempted to break loose as Kyle was still passionately kissing her, and breathlessly said, "No, I can't do this, Kyle, I have to go."

As she started to run, a confused Kyle called after her, "Elea!"

She quickly made her way back to the dorm, breathless and shaking. When she reached the inside of the building, she stood up against the door, panting.

"Hey, are you okay?" Scott asked, confused, as he looked up from the table where he was enjoying a late dinner.

She glanced over at him, shook her head, couldn't respond, tried to compose herself, then proceeded into her room and started to ready herself for her time away from Scarlet Oak Valley.

As she packed her suitcase, still shaking, she felt guilty of the emotions swirling within her. At that moment, she felt clearly torn between this very handsome man with a young son and her boyfriend of several years.

Judy S. Wagner

CHAPTER 11

ELEA HOPPED THE TRAIN HEADED for Metro Line City, New York, a busy city with a huge population. As she stared out of the window, her thoughts were consumed with the moment she shared with Kyle the night before. He was so handsome and desirable. She wished things could have been different where he wasn't keeping company with the church assistant, and where she wasn't already involved in a long-term relationship.

She thought of the passionate kiss both had shared on his porch, and how she wished that kiss would've never ended. Kyle appeared not to want it to end, but she had to face the reality of making it end due to her relationship ties to her boyfriend.

Elea arrived at the train station in Metro Line City and hailed a cab. Throughout the cab ride to Selene's apartment, she couldn't help but notice the difference between life in the busy city, versus the laid-back rural country environment where she spent the past few months. She loved the weather and the warm southern hospitality in Scarlet Oak Valley. Selene had gone away to Vermont for the holiday season. She had previously given Elea a key to her apartment, and welcomed her to take advantage of the space.

When Elea settled in, she phoned Lane. Once again, no response. So she left a voicemail message. By 4:00 p.m. the following afternoon, he returned her call. Elea had gone out shopping. When she returned, she took note of his voicemail message.

"Hey, Elea, it's me. I knew you were headed this way for the holidays. I'm at the tail end of the ski trip I took to Colorado with a bunch of my associates. We should be headed back to town in another day or two. I'd ask you to return my call, but I have no idea where I'll be."

As she listened to his message, her heart sank. She couldn't quite target the "tone". He didn't even say he missed her. There was no warmth in his voice. She thought they would connect starting from when she first arrived back in the city. She clearly felt let down. *So he took a ski trip to Colorado with friends when he knew I was expected home yesterday,* she pondered.

When Lane returned two days later, he and Elea made plans to meet for dinner at an upscale city restaurant. Since it was the holiday season, most venues were crowded. Despite the reservations he made for them, there were still long waiting lines. Once seated in the restaurant, the waiter took their drink order. Elea and Lane ordered dinner and the waiter proceeded to collect their menus. After dinner and an uneventful conversation, they exited the restaurant. They strolled over to Lane's BMW, got in, and headed to a local nightclub for additional drinks.

As they took seats at the bar, Elea faced him, "Lane, I have been waiting for so long to see you. I've really missed you! I'm so happy we'll have these next two weeks together!"

He smiled, took a sip of his bourbon, and then faced downward, "Yeah, it's good to see you, too, Elea." Something didn't quite sound right.

He tried to avoid her eyes as best as he could, then added, "I need to talk to you."

She replied, "Sure, Lane, anything in particular?"

Lane explained, "I'm sorry that I can't be spending time with you while you're up here visiting. The firm wants me to fly out to California tomorrow morning for a business conference. I'll be on the west coast for the next month."

He noted her genuine look of surprise and disappointment. He continued, "Sorry, Elea, it doesn't mean that I don't love you; it's just that I can't be available throughout the time you're visiting."

Elea responded, "Funny, I thought that when I planned this trip, and mainly from how you spoke, you were really looking forward to my visit. You said that we would be spending a lot of time together. I understand that you're busy with work, Lane, but I was really looking forward to us being together, and thought you had already put in for some vacation time."

Lane continued, "I still love you, Elea, but there's distance that's come between us now since you became involved in that outreach ministry. And with me needing to frequently fly out to different cities, I suggest we keep our dating options open."

Elea sat shocked and motionless. She couldn't breathe. "Lane, I don't understand why we can't keep our relationship exclusive, despite our crazy schedules."

He faced downward and took another sip of his drink. "But you even said, Elea, that after this outreach assignment in Tennessee ends, you volunteers will be recruited into working in other parts of the country. It's like I'm in a relationship with a missionary. That will make it especially hard for us to be together, I hope you realize that."

Elea heaved a huge sigh and sat back. She totally understood Lane's perspective. He was right. She sadly nodded, then spoke words she never imagined possible.

"Lane, it means so much to me that we stay together that I would even give up this outreach volunteering. I would do it only if I knew you wanted to keep the relationship exclusive between us, and relinquish the idea of us seeing other people."

How horrible she felt once she spoke those words, and immediately regretted having said them. The reality was that she just could never imagine herself NOT volunteering to help less fortunate people. She also couldn't believe she sounded like she was "begging" Lane to reconsider.

He responded, "I'm not sure of what I want right now, Elea. I suggest we both keep our minds open to dating others. We'll stay in touch and see what happens going forward." He spoke those words as if he had already made his decision.

She sadly responded, "It sounds like your mind is made up, Lane. That's fine if that's what you want to do."

But it really wasn't fine. They had been going together since their college days, and had formed a wonderful relationship bond throughout their many years together.

There were no other words left to say. Lane obviously preferred to have an open relationship. He dropped Elea off to Selene's apartment. Lane promised he would connect with her by the following spring season to reassess things between them. In the back of her mind, Elea somehow doubted she would hear from him.

Once alone in the apartment, she sat depressed. She perked up a bit when Selene phoned her from the ski lodge in Vermont to wish her a Merry Christmas and a Happy New Year. Selene was employed as a financial analyst in the city and was working on her graduate degree in the evening. She and Elea had been best friends since high school.

Elea asked, "When are you flying back in, Selene?"

Her friend responded, "I should be there the day before New Year's. Why, did you want to go out on New Year's Eve?"

"Yes, I would love that!" exclaimed Elea, "And dinner and drinks are on me," she added.

It was New Year's Eve in the city when Selene and Elea dressed up to go out. The cab picked them up. They ate dinner, and then they visited a popular dance club in the heart of the city. They claimed seats at the bar and chatted. Elea informed her of what had happened with Lane. Selene wasn't surprised. For that matter, neither was Elea.

She explained to Selene, "Scott said he thought Lane was seeing other women. I just didn't want to face that reality. When he wasn't returning my calls, I knew in the back of my mind something just wasn't right. I became depressed over it, but 'something' happened recently with someone else when I was ministering in Scarlet Oak Valley. It was something that clearly caused a distraction, and made me question now whether my feelings for Lane were ever legitimate."

Elea proceeded to tell Selene all about Kyle, his son Jack, and the unexpected kiss. She continued, "I felt guilty when it happened and instantly broke away, but I really wanted him to kiss me."

Selene responded, "I'm sure he wouldn't have done it if he wasn't feeling something for you, Elea."

Elea continued, "He supposedly has a girlfriend. She's Reverend Ward's assistant. She's not a very nice person, yet has a lot of influence in that church. I understood from the former choir director that she could make life tough on people she doesn't care for. And I know she and her clique of friends don't care for me. Gosh, can you imagine if she knew her guy kissed me? Now I have a challenge to face when I return there. I'll have to keep my distance from him, as well, which will be difficult. His kiss was totally amazing!"

Selene replied, "Hear me out, girlfriend, been there, done that. When a man sets his sights on you and is determined to have you, nothing or no one can change his mind. I'm sure you'll be fine. Relax and take each day as it comes."

The second week of January arrived. Elea bid her best friend goodbye and boarded the train headed back to Scarlet Oak Valley. She was anxiously looking forward to resuming her volunteer work, and seeing Kyle and Jack again.

"Happy New Year, Elea!" excitedly greeted Scott, as Elea walked into the dorm. The two friends embraced. Scott asked, "So, how was your time with Lane?"

Elea's face grew sad. She set her suitcase down, took off her coat, hung it up, turned to face Scott, but didn't respond. He noticed.

Elea replied, "Let me get organized and we can talk over some coffee, Scott." After Elea unpacked and got settled back in, she and Scott took seats at the table and started to catch up.

Elea stated, "Well, it just seemed so strange that he didn't even act like he was happy to see me. We hugged after dinner and he said he would connect with me in the spring, but it was just weird."

She went on to explain to Scott the conversation she and Lane had and his suggestion that they date other people, yet still continue with their relationship.

She added, "He'll be traveling a lot. He explained that he feels like he's in a relationship with a missionary. He also emphasized the distance that will make it difficult for us to see each other. If two people want to stay together, Scott, couldn't they find a way to make it work? I even found myself offering to give up the ministry if he agreed to keep our relationship exclusive."

Scott replied, "Elea, you've been used to an exciting life with him when you lived in the city. You got caught up in the bright lights, went to the dance clubs, theaters, rode in his BMW and dined at the most expensive restaurants. You wore jewelry he bought for you that cost a fortune, and there wasn't anything you wanted that he wasn't getting for you. Would you miss all of that if you continued with this ministry?"

Elea stared at him, glanced downward, looked up and shook her head. "Do you want the truth? No, not for a minute." Once again, she considered Kyle and their kiss, but wouldn't allow herself to share that private information with Scott.

Elea continued, "I don't think I'll have that choice to make, Scott. It's very doubtful I'll ever hear from Lane again."

On the other hand, Kyle lived in a small, modest home, wore jeans, open flannel shirts and color t-shirts, and needed to watch his budget. He was a few years older than Elea, was in his early thirties, and had a young child for which to provide. He was working on his Doctor of Theology degree. He was the complete opposite of Lane. Materialism wasn't what he was all about.

As Elea dreamed of Kyle's warm embrace, she was excited to resume her volunteer work in Scarlet Oak Valley. She also looked forward to resuming her child sitter responsibilities with Jack. Elea enjoyed her's and Jack's evenings together and the close bond they had formed. And she always looked forward to Kyle's gorgeous smile and tender looks whenever she left his house after child sitting.

Elea felt she needed to talk to Kyle and fully explain to him why she had run off. Things last ended awkwardly between them once she broke loose of his grip as he was passionately kissing her.

Once the day's activities with helping the senior women with food shopping ended, she bundled up and took a walk over to Kyle's. It was early evening. He answered the door, looking a bit confused and showing a little indifference.

"Hi," he greeted her with a surprised look, his gorgeous piercing light green eyes focused seriously on her.

Elea asked, "Can I talk to you?"

Kyle stepped outside. He folded his arms and looked downward, then faced her and asked, "Where've you been? Jack was asking for you last Wednesday night. I told him I didn't know where you were. Then when I heard you had left for two weeks, I was surprised you didn't say anything. I let him know and he was really disappointed."

Elea replied, "Can I talk to Jack? I apologize for not having said anything, but I'm here now. It's a long story which I'll need to explain. Wasn't the Wednesday night bible study and choir practice supposed to resume this coming Wednesday?"

Kyle faced downward, "No, both of those events resumed LAST Wednesday night. I guess you didn't check the church calendar. Besides, now isn't a good time, Elea. And I probably won't be needing you to child sit for him in the future. Beth and I discussed, and we feel it's best to recruit a responsible teen from our ministry. This person can also keep an eye on him when she and I go out. Plus, you're overwhelmed with your volunteer responsibilities. From speaking with Scott, you and your group will become even more overwhelmed with other projects."

"I hope you know just how much I looked forward to my Wednesday nights with Jack. And I would still love to spend time with him." Elea sadly replied, as she stared into Kyle's handsome face.

Beth then poked her head out the door, "I thought I heard voices out here."

When she saw it was Elea that Kyle was speaking with, she grew serious. She then grinned with satisfaction as she stared at Elea, "Whenever you're ready, Kyle, we can have our dinner and talk about plans." And with that said, she closed the door.

Elea felt nauseous. *I wonder what kind of plans,* she thought. She continued, "I'm sorry, Kyle, I didn't mean to run off like that. I'll need to explain why, but it's definitely not what you thought."

He stood staring at her with folded arms and with the same serious look on his face. He coldly responded, "It's not important. I have to go inside now, Elea; we're getting ready to eat. I don't want to keep Beth and Jack waiting."

It was obvious he was very upset with her. He proceeded to step back inside the house and didn't even wait until she walked down the front porch steps. As she watched him walk back into his home and close the door, a tear streamed down her cheek. She helplessly stood alone, then sadly made her way back to the dorm.

CHAPTER 12

"HEY, HAPPY YOU COULD MAKE it here, buddy, how was your trip?" Kyle asked his friend and former roommate, Brent Somerville. "Come in, let's have a drink," Kyle added, as he welcomed Brent into his home.

Brent was Kyle's best friend and roommate when both started their studies in divinity college. Brent was a native of Oregon who had planned a visit to see Kyle and Jack early in the New Year.

The two friends sat and talked that evening. "So, let me get this straight, you're going with Beth, the church assistant?" Brent asked.

Kyle nodded and replied, "We date, yes. Actually, we just recruited a volunteer from our teen ministry to help with Jack on Wednesday nights. The same sitter will also watch Jack when Beth and I go out."

For a moment, Kyle looked pensive. He thought of how Elea sat with his son, and how thrilled Jack was whenever they spent time together.

The subject of the outreach volunteer workers came up. Kyle explained to Brent the role they were playing in the small church and community.

"Sounds like they're really helping your congregation," Brent replied, "I would love to have good people like them working in my church when I eventually become pastor."

"Everett will make introductions after this Sunday's services at the hospitality hour. You can meet them then," Kyle assured his friend.

The following Sunday morning, Reverend Ward introduced Brent Somerville to the small congregation following services. He informed everyone that Brent was a friend of Kyle's who was in town to visit for a few weeks. Brent had arrived shortly after the New Year. He would be departing by the end of February. During his short visit with Kyle, Brent spoke with Reverend Ward, inquired about the volunteers, and even offered his assistance to them.

Elea spotted Jack walking back from the refreshment table and stooped to greet him. At first he looked sad and had some difficulty facing her.

"Jack, how are you? I'm really sorry I had to go away during the Christmas holidays, but hoped you liked the present I left for you." He didn't respond, but merely looked down. Elea felt bad.

"Thank you for the present, Miss Elea, but why did you go?" he asked, appearing confused, as he shyly glanced up at her.

"Oh honey, I was going to explain why to your dad, but … ."

At that moment, Kyle, Beth and Brent were approaching them. Elea stood up and Jack continued walking over to a table of his friends. Elea faced Kyle, Beth and Brent as they gradually approached her.

"Who's the dish? Introduce me," Brent insisted, as he focused on Elea, "wow, is she pretty!"

Beth insisted, as well, "Yes, Kyle, DO introduce Brent to 'the dish'."

Kyle, feeling helpless, frowned, as he glanced at both of them. Elea started to turn and walk away. "Elea, do you have a second?" Kyle called after her.

"Yeah, sure … " she replied with hesitation as she faced him, Beth and Brent.

"I'd like for you to meet my best friend and roommate from divinity college, Brent Somerville. He's visiting for the month from Oregon." Elea extended her hand as she politely faced Brent.

"The best looking women obviously come from the northern part of this country. Hi, I'm Brent," he said, as he flashed a sexy smile, and firmly shook Elea's hand. He added, "I would love to chat sometime."

Elea was impressed with Brent's friendliness, good looks and charm. She met his gaze and smiled, flattered by his nice, complimentive words.

Brent suggested, "Let's go get some coffee and chat about your outreach ministry. I'm very interested in learning more about it." Elea smiled and let Brent escort her to the refreshment table.

Feelings of jealousy he had never felt before entered into Kyle as he stood, observing the interaction between his friend and woman for whom he had developed feelings. He felt helpless, yet needed to maintain his strength and composure. It was abundantly clear Elea was impressed with his best friend and vice-versa.

Beth put her arm around Kyle's waist and was beaming. "Looks like a great match!" she said as she looked up at Kyle, "They look so perfect together."

Kyle continued to stare at them. Feelings of nausea were now starting to set in. He especially wasn't happy when Brent put his arm around Elea's waist, and insisted she walk him over and introduce him to Scott and to the rest of the volunteers. Elea seemed pleased to accommodate him. Brent certainly seemed to be working his charm on her.

Kyle frowned, walked over to get his son, and left the fellowship hall with Beth and Jack, rather disgusted.

"Hey Kyle, I was talking with Elea. I told her we should go out sometime with you and Beth before I have to head back," Brent suggested as he took a seat in the church office.

Kyle was busy working in Reverend Ward's office on the church's finances. He stopped, leaned back in his chair, ran his hand through his hair, and faced his friend with his usual serious look.

"So what's going on with you and Elea?" he needed to ask Brent.

Brent smiled and responded, "I don't know, but I think I may want to get to know her better."

Kyle suddenly started coughing, and had to take a sip of the bottled water that was sitting on his desk. "Oh really?" he frowned, shaking his head, hoping he hadn't heard Brent speaking those words.

Brent continued, "Why not? She told me her investment broker boyfriend in the city had gone skiing with a group of his associates during the Christmas holidays and how … ."

Kyle suddenly interrupted him, looking confused, "Wait. What investment broker boyfriend? Is she going with a guy back home?"

Brent replied, "Apparently so. She said he was her boyfriend since college. They made plans to meet up during the Christmas holidays for two weeks, and she felt confident he would be proposing. As it turned out, he told her he had gone skiing with a group of his associates during the break. He told her that he still wanted to date her, but wasn't ready to seriously commit due to her ministry here and his traveling schedule. He suggested they date other people. I know Elea was upset about it. I think he told her he would contact her by spring time."

Kyle felt bad for what had happened to Elea. *No wonder she ran from me ...* he thought as he stared down at the desk. It started to make sense now as to why Elea broke loose from his arms and quickly ran as they were kissing. It was a matter of her being loyal to her boyfriend back home. His mind thought back to Christmas night when they passionately kissed, and how she suddenly broke loose from his embrace. He was confused and hurt. He was confused as to why she ran from him. When she didn't return to watch Jack on the Wednesday night for which she was scheduled, his hurt turned to anger. Beth, at that point, convinced Kyle that he should consider someone from the teen ministry to take on the responsibility of child sitting for Jack. She emphasized that Elea was much too irresponsible. Still hurt, confused and angry at the time, he concurred with Beth's way of thinking.

Kyle regained his composure and replied, "Listen, Brent, you just got here. I suggest you take things slow. After all, she and her boyfriend sound like they're still in some kind of a relationship."

Brent shrugged and replied, "Well, we're going out tonight to see a movie. There isn't too much to do in this quaint town of yours, is there? Even Elea was saying how much she missed the bright city lights, clubs, theaters, and the crowded sidewalks of Metro Line City. She said it's especially beautiful during the holiday season."

Kyle sadly nodded and thought, *"I'm sure she does miss all of those things."*

When Brent closed the door behind him, Kyle sat back and continued thinking, *I'm sure this town can't even compare to what she's been used to.* He looked melancholy for a minute, ran his hand again through his hair, and then forced himself to settle down into his finance work. However, thoughts of the night he kissed Elea were still swirling around in his head.

"Hey Brent, I haven't seen much of you since you've been here," Kyle mentioned to his friend, as Brent walked through the church doors late one night. Kyle had still been hard at work on the church's finances. When he heard Brent entering, he got up from the desk in his office, rubbed his eyes, yawned and stretched.

Brent replied, "Elea and I went for a drive. It gets really dark around these parts. She's so great, buddy. We went out for dinner, had ice cream, and then explored more of the town. I'm really enjoying her company."

Despite his fatigue, Kyle stood staring at him and feeling envious, as he listened to Brent recap his date with Elea.

Brent again suggested, "Why don't you, Beth, Elea and I double date one night?"

Kyle frowned and responded, "I don't know, Brent, I'll need a sitter for Jack."

Brent asked, "Didn't you say you recruited a sitter for when you and Beth date?"

Kyle nodded and responded, "We recently recruited Mrs. Kelly's teenage daughter to keep an eye on him. Not the ideal situation, as I was hoping not to have a teenager look after him. I suppose the four of us could go out one night," Kyle responded with reservation.

Brent replied, "We should. I only have another week to be here, and then need to head back to Oregon and continue on with school."

Both Kyle and Brent were working on that same Doctor of Theology degree, while serving as associate pastors in their respective congregations.

CHAPTER 13

FEBRUARY WAS THE MONTH OF Valentine's Day. Scott, Elea, their volunteers, the teen ministry and church members were enthusiastically hard at work. They were decorating the fellowship hall with joyful red, pink and white valentine hearts, along with other tasteful decorations, for the church Valentine dance that evening.

"Need some help?" Brent asked Elea, as he and Kyle stepped into the hall.

"Yes, if you have time," Elea smiled at them, "You're both welcome to give us a hand." Brent smiled, and Kyle just stood staring at her with folded arms.

Elea asked one of the church members for a ladder. She proceeded to climb up to fix one of the red paper heart decorations that was becoming undone from the ceiling. Brent and Kyle rolled up their sleeves and started to help everyone. Both were in close proximity to where Elea was working on the ladder.

"Oh gosh, this ladder is shaky," she suddenly said, and then felt the ladder wobbling, as she was ready to slip off. Kyle noticed and raced over to her, barely catching her in his arms. By then, all of the volunteers had stopped what they were doing and ran over to where they were.

Kyle tightly hugged Elea's trembling body and asked, "Are you okay?" as he stared into her eyes. She was caught up again in the moment staring straight into his piercing light eyes.

Still shaking, she glanced away, focused downward and nodded, "Yes, thanks…" and then he released her.

"I'll fix whatever you were trying to do up there," he added.

Elea, a little breathless, replied, "Thank you." Kyle proceeded up the ladder and adjusted the loose decoration.

That evening, the hall looked festive and fun. The same local DJ was recruited to provide music, and a pot-luck supper was provided by all of the church members. Everyone was eagerly looking forward to a great time. The outreach volunteers, adult church members and teen ministry entered the fellowship hall an hour prior to the dance. They arranged everything in order. The buffet and dessert tables were set up. The various eight-seat round tables were covered with red and white plastic tablecloths, with pink, white and red glitter sprinkled over each table, and tasteful heart-shaped candle centerpieces.

Kyle, Beth, Brent and Reverend Ward entered the hall. Jack was with them, as well, and was fascinated by the festive decorations as he stared at the surroundings. They all took seats at a table in the front. Scott sat with half of their volunteers at a table in the back, close to the buffet area, and Elea sat with the rest of the volunteers at the table next to them.

Reverend Ward stepped up to the microphone where the DJ had set up, asked all to bow their heads in prayer, welcomed everyone, and graciously thanked the volunteers for hosting the event.

The DJ announced that the buffet dinner was ready. All volunteers left their tables and stationed themselves to accommodate the congregation as they formed lines and took dinner plates. Beth shot Elea a dirty look. She followed Kyle, Brent, Jack and Reverend Ward as they sauntered up to the buffet line.

As Kyle was following behind his son, guiding him back to their table, he quietly smiled and acknowledged Elea. Brent smiled and winked at her as he followed behind them. All of the volunteers patiently waited until everyone in the congregation was served, and then they helped themselves to their own meals.

Dancing followed next and continued throughout the evening. Elea had many offers to dance from various-aged males in attendance. She graciously danced with several of the male members of the congregation, and even engaged in popular dance routines with many of the female teens. Brent occupied a lot of her time on the dance floor, as well. He apparently was a great dancer, was a very outgoing guy, and loved to party.

As Elea and Brent ended one slow dance and the DJ was about to play another, Elea took note of how Jack sat alongside of his dad, still appearing shy and observing his surroundings.

Elea excused herself from Brent, walked over to Jack and asked, "Excuse me, may I please dance with this very handsome young man?" she smiled, as she faced him.

Kyle seemed grateful and replied, "How about it buddy? Miss Elea would like to dance with you."

Jack shyly glanced downward, yet seemed pleased and said, "Okay".

"Of course," Elea responded, as she walked over to lead him from the table onto the dance floor. Beth sat there seething as she watched Kyle's mesmerized face as he was observing Elea and his young son happily dancing.

"Let's dance, Kyle!" she insisted, as she pulled his hand and dragged him onto the dance floor, "And why do you keep looking at them when you're supposed to be here with me?" she added in an angry tone. Beth wasn't happy, as she pushed herself into Kyle's chest.

When he faced her, she stopped dancing, grabbed hold of his arms, put them around her waist, and then made sure she passionately kissed him. Elea did a double-take as she danced with Jack, and glanced over just in time to catch the action. She was shocked. The song then ended. Kyle noted the look of astonishment on Elea's face.

As she was walking Jack back to the table, the DJ once again started playing another slow song. Kyle broke loose from Beth and called Elea's name. Elea had seated Jack back at the table and turned to face Kyle. "Will you dance with me?" he asked.

Elea hesitated, as she caught fire from Beth's facial expression. "I don't know if that's a good idea..."

"I insist, let's dance," Kyle stated with determination as he took charge and pulled Elea back onto the dance floor. The lights darkened in the hall as the last slow dance of the evening was being played.

Kyle held Elea close to him as they danced, "Thanks for dancing with my son. I know he appreciated being asked," he said, staring into her eyes, "By the way, are you okay from that incident with the ladder today?" he half chuckled, holding her tight while still staring into her eyes.

"If you hadn't been there to catch me, maybe tonight would've been a different story," she replied with a chuckle and a sigh of relief.

Kyle felt the urge to just stop dancing and wanted to kiss Elea. He focused on her lips and was very close to kissing her when Beth rudely positioned herself between them and broke them apart.

"I'd like to dance with MY date!" she exclaimed with disgust as she scowled at Elea.

"Of course," Elea replied.

It was a very awkward moment for all three of them. Elea glanced downward, suddenly feeling ashamed of herself for having shared such a warm dance with Kyle. However, Beth was right in that Kyle was HER date for the evening.

"That was a great event last night! Valentine's Day itself is coming up this Saturday, and that will be a perfect time to go on a double date," Brent stated the next day, as he and Kyle were having lunch in Kyle's church office.

Kyle once again looked apprehensive. He wondered if that particular holiday meant for love would be such a good idea. He especially thought of the previous evening. He was pre-occupied thinking of Elea's sweetness with asking his son to dance, as well as his own romantic dance with her. Warm thoughts of her swirled around in his head. If Beth hadn't interrupted their dance, he couldn't trust himself that his lips would've been kissing Elea's.

Elea was apprehensive, as well, when Brent proposed the idea. She, too, thought of the church dance and how she wished she could've remained in Kyle's arms.

"I don't think Kyle's girlfriend is fond of me, Brent. She's been treating our volunteers, and especially me, very rudely since we arrived." She looked concerned as she faced him, "The four of us going out together on

Valentine's Day evening is probably not a good idea. Maybe just you and I should go out that night."

Sensing some kind of an issue, Brent agreed, as he didn't want to fuel any fires.

Valentine's Day evening arrived and Brent picked up Elea for their date. She looked lovely in an attractive red dress and matching accessories. Her beautiful long brown hair flowed. They proceeded to go to dinner in the local town.

Brent asked, "So what's going on now with Kyle's girlfriend not caring for you? She's probably jealous of you."

Elea replied, "Our volunteers and I were never out to make peoples' lives uncomfortable," she explained, "I have respect knowing Beth and Kyle date. I'm sure he has serious feelings for her. She was alluding about them 'making plans' so I would assume they're in a serious relationship."

Deep inside, Elea was dying and wishing it wasn't so. She was confused. In one sense, she knew Kyle and Beth were dating. In another sense, Kyle's body language kept strongly revealing otherwise. She especially recalled that he was on the brink of kissing her during that final slow dance.

Brent listened intently to Elea's thoughts on Kyle and Beth. His own thoughts wandered for a minute as he became distracted, *This is very interesting, I wonder if Beth is jealous of this beauty because she might sense some attraction between her and Kyle?*

Brent was curious, "Had you and Kyle ever dated?"

Elea responded, "No, I think everyone at the church knows he's been dating Beth for the past three years."

Elea dared not tell him about the night when Kyle passionately kissed her on his porch. That remained her secret alone. The only other person who knew was her Metro Line City friend, Selene.

Brent replied, "Kyle wasn't all that fond of the idea of us all going out, either." He paused, then added, "I think I can see what's going on here."

Elea responded, "It will be interesting to know what kind of 'plans' Beth and Kyle will be making. But let's not talk about them anymore and just enjoy our date."

Elea smiled, desiring to no longer stay on that same topic of discussion. Brent understood and nodded.

The next day, Brent opened the door to the church office and found Kyle still working on the church's financial spreadsheet.

Kyle looked up and asked, "Hey buddy, what's up?"

Brent asked, "How was your evening last night? What did you and Beth do?"

Kyle replied, "Went to dinner and I gave her flowers."

"Nothing else?" Brent questioned, expecting to hear more of a response.

Kyle faced his friend, appearing confused, "Uh, no, was there supposed to be something else?"

Brent responded, "How long have you been dating Beth? No jewelry, no engagement ring?"

At that point, Kyle sat back in his chair and faced his friend with wide eyes. He wondered all of a sudden why his friend was asking so many questions. He frowned, "No, there's been nothing promised to her. Why do you ask?"

Brent replied, "Are you and Beth making any plans?"

Kyle stared at him with a look of confusion and asked, "What plans? I have no immediate plans of becoming engaged to her or to anyone else, if that's what you mean. My son is my primary responsibility. Besides, I would always make sure that it would be something HE would want, as well."

"Have you communicated that to her?" Brent asked.

Kyle responded, "No, I don't find that necessary. Beth and I just go out on dates, and she sometimes helps with Jack."

Brent's immediate thought was, *Apparently this Beth seems to think Kyle's just as serious about her as she is about him and may be expecting too much.*

"How about you, what did you do last night?" Kyle asked Brent, as he faced his paperwork and started to check some figures.

"I took Elea out. She's a very sweet woman and we had a great dinner and conversation," Brent responded.

Kyle paused from what he was doing and looked up at his friend.

"Oh, so you're still seeing her," he replied with a tone of sadness in his voice. Those feelings of envy were starting to surface again. This time, Brent noticed.

"Yes, I like her a lot. Too bad I have to leave for Oregon in a few days. But she and I will be staying in touch. There's a possibility she and her outreach volunteers may head into our state and serve the community where I'm associate pastor. How I would look forward to seeing her once they arrive at our church. I'm still not convinced about the boyfriend from back home bit."

After Brent left the office, Kyle sat back again deep in thought, *So now my best buddy apparently has feelings for her and intends to stay in touch with her. And one day she could also be volunteering in his church community.*

The end of February arrived and Brent was scheduled to depart for Oregon to resume his doctoral studies. He loaded his suitcases in his car and waited until Kyle stepped out of the house to see him off.

He thanked Kyle for his hospitality, then spoke, "Hey guy, listen up, about Elea. If you have feelings for that beautiful woman, I would suggest you let her know. Otherwise, someone else will scoop her up before you've had that opportunity, and then you will

have lost her. Just something for you to think about."
Brent winked and patted Kyle on the back.

"Thanks," Kyle replied.

He stood serious as he shook Brent's hand and
wished him all the best. He added, "Take care of
yourself, buddy." He waved as Brent drove away.

The six-month outreach assignment was coming to an
end. Scott, Elea and the volunteers were in question as
to where their next assignment would take place. As
they all stood discussing one morning, Reverend Ward
called a meeting in his office with the two coordinators.

"Come in, come in," he welcomed them, as he
smiled and greeted Scott and Elea. They entered and
took seats across from him.

"I just wanted to let you know that I've spoken
to Father Bud to report on the progress you and your
volunteers have been making in our church and this
community. I also called a meeting with our church's
senior deacons. Everyone unanimously agreed that you
and your volunteers should continue working in our
community for an additional six months. Would you
consider staying with us for that time? And Scott, you
mentioned that Father Bud said, if need be, it's possible
your time here could even extend to a limit of eighteen
months?" Reverend Ward asked.

"Yes, he did, Reverend Ward, but would you think you'll need us for a complete eighteen months?"

Scott needed to ask, as he and Elea had previously discussed it last Thanksgiving Day. He knew her feelings with regard to Kyle and Beth.

Reverend Ward responded, "We could revisit after these next six months. However, the good news is that you and your volunteers are adding such blessings to our little community that, to be honest, we would hate to see you leave right now. Do I have your word you'll stay with us for an additional six months?" He looked concerned and hoped Scott and Elea would agree.

"Yes, of course, we'll be happy to continue with our volunteer work here at the church. We'll gather all of our workers together to let them know we won't be going anywhere for a while yet. They love it here and I'm sure they'll all be pleased you feel we're doing such a great job," Scott responded, as Elea forced a smile and nodded.

Reverend Ward noticed Elea's lack of enthusiasm. "Elea, is this okay with you, as well?"

She replied, "Sure, Reverend Ward, we'll be happy to stay on and continue with our volunteer work here." But she genuinely wasn't sure.

Immediate thoughts surfaced regarding Kyle and Beth, how Beth would react to the news, and would still continue to harass her. Many times Elea considered having a one-on-one discussion with Beth to attempt to settle any strife and hard feelings between them. It was difficult because Beth wouldn't even be civil to Elea, much less be willing to talk over differences. Since Beth was perpetually rude to her, Elea buried the thought of a discussion. Instead, she tolerated Beth's bad behavior, prayed for her, and prayed that her attitude would change.

She also didn't trust her feelings and how devastated she would be if and when she heard that Kyle would propose to Beth, as Beth always made that point abundantly clear. They had been dating shortly after Kyle's wife, Haley, had passed. Their relationship started three years ago, and Beth would in no way ever allow Kyle to remain out of her sight and control.

Judy S. Wagner

CHAPTER 14

S COTT, ELEA, AND THE VOLUNTEERS continued their hard-work efforts within the small community. By then, Elea had made many friends among the adult members of the congregation, and among the teen ministry members. They had shown much enthusiasm at project meetings. The active teen ministry even presented fresh new helpful ideas of their own. She even noticed a remarkable change in Avalene, who was one of Beth's friends, and Ariana's mother. Ariana was the little girl who Elea had selected to play the role of Mary in the Christmas pageant.

Avalene became one of Elea's best church volunteers and even asked to head the Easter Egg Hunt. Avalene formed a small committee of her fellow church members. She met with Scott, Elea, and the volunteers with regard to the budget and what purchases would be the most affordable for the event. Avalene and her committee took the lead in the organization of the many indoor Easter decorations. The teen ministry members worked in conjunction with her committee in the planning of a simple continental breakfast on

Easter Sunday morning. The breakfast would include homemade donuts and pastries, various flavored juices and coffee and tea. Two separate tables were arranged in the back of the room for food and drink items, in addition to the paper good products and utensils.

Elea and Avalene headed to the local discount store to purchase the necessary items for the egg hunt, which would be held on the Saturday afternoon prior to Easter, right on the church grounds. Baskets of small, inexpensive prizes were purchased. Trophies would be presented to the winners of the three different categories: Most Eggs, Fewest Eggs, and a Good Egg. At the egg hunt, everyone chuckled as the Reverend Ward received a small trophy for being "a Good Egg".

The evening before the Easter holiday, the fellowship hall was festively decorated with colorful Easter egg string lights, Bunny balloons, egg wreaths, eggshell garland, and a mini egg tree. Long tables were covered with pink and purple pastel plastic tablecloths, mason jars in springtime colors with Easter egg designs, and bunches of yellow, pink, purple, blue and green pastel balloons at each table.

On Easter Sunday morning, following services, as the church members made their way downstairs, the fellowship hall looked festive and delightful and put smiles on everyones' faces.

Elea stepped up to the podium and welcomed everyone, wishing all a very Happy Easter and a Happy Springtime. She had been hard at work helping Avalene, the teen ministry, Scott and all the volunteers and church members in putting the final touches to the fellowship hall. Everyone was seated at their tables and focused on her as she was about ready to continue her welcome greeting. As she glanced around the room, she took note of Reverend Ward sitting at a back table with Kyle, Beth and Jack.

"Once again, I would like to welcome you all and thank Avalene and her wonderful committee of volunteers, our teen ministry, all of those church members who worked so hard and generously gave up their time to help us, and Scott and our own volunteers. Without all of you, this event would not have been possible. So thank you, everyone." Elea smiled graciously, amid smiles and applause from the congregation. And with that being said, she took a seat with Scott and the volunteers.

Beth quickly got out of her seat and asked Avalene to step outside with her. A few moments later, Elea realized she had left her purse at the dorm and needed to walk over to the building to grab it. As she opened the door to exit fellowship hall, she overheard Beth talking to Avalene. They were standing on the other side of the trash bins, but she could hear every word.

"I can't believe you let yourself be on HER committee to plan this! I thought we were friends! You, yourself, said you couldn't stand her when that group first came to us last summer, so why are you being so nice to her now?" Beth stated, as she read Avalene the riot act.

Avalene responded, "Beth, I think you're all wrong about her. She's so nice, and she and her workers are all doing a great job for this church. I may not have liked Elea when I first met her, but I like her a lot now."

Beth frowned, rolled her eyes, and threw her hands up in the air. The door made a sound as Elea stepped out of the building and was in view.

Realizing Elea was in close proximity, Beth purposely informed Avalene, "I have a secret to tell you. Kyle said he loves me and said he promises we'll get engaged by this Christmas. He told me so right after the holidays last year. It was the second week of January to be exact. I might even be moving in with him and Jack."

Elea's heart sank. She was both shaken and saddened by overhearing those words. Elea remembered that night. It was when she returned from Metro Line City and had stopped over to try to explain to Kyle why she ran from him. He was obviously upset with her that night, and it showed. She wondered if it was on that evening when he made such a promise to Beth. This time, Beth genuinely sounded serious and positive that it would happen.

Elea put her head down and started to slowly walk in the direction of the dorm. *I guess maybe what I'm not understanding is if he feels that way about her, and all of this is going to happen with them, why am I getting different messages from him?*

Though Beth's words devastated her, that night Elea prayed and gave it all up to the Lord. She recalled the words of a very special friend from her own church in Metro Line City, *"If you put God first in your life, you can get through anything."*

It was April, and the spring season rolled in. It was a time of rebirth, renewal, rejuvenation, and regrowth. It was the blossoming of ranges of plant species, activities of animals, and the smell of soil. Due to the hemisphere beginning to warm significantly, new plant growth began to spring forth. Snow started to melt, and swelling streams with runoff became less severe. Many flowering plants were blooming at this time of year, sometimes beginning with snow still on the ground and continuing into the early summer months.

Springtime meant the preparation of flower and vegetable gardens for the senior community. Gardening tools needed to be purchased, such as seed syringes, seed tape and seed with the soil mixed in. Tree and hedge trimming, mulching, lawn mowing, weed pulling, setting up a drip irrigation system, and preparing beds for planting in areas of landscape, were some of the projects that lie ahead.

Major clean-up efforts were also begun in the many seniors' yards following the mild winter season that year. Dead tree limbs and branches were clipped out and bushes were trimmed. The volunteers took trips to local garden and home improvement stores in the hopes of aiding the seniors with the planting of flower and vegetable gardens and landscaping. Lawn maintenance, house painting, and other outside tasks were undertaken by not only the volunteers, but by eager-to-help church members.

Years ago, the congregation created a vegetable garden in a neglected corner of the grounds. However, due to lack of funds, they were unable to maintain it. Elea, Scott and the volunteers suggested resurrecting the vegetable garden in the month of May. The church members agreed it was a wonderful idea.

Easy-to-grow veggies like cucumbers, squash and lettuce could even be shared with the local food pantry. Milkweed seeds could be grown and then replanted as a host plant for threatened monarch butterflies. In addition, areas could be prepared for spring vegetable crops, such as broccoli, cabbage, peas, spinach, lettuce, onions, potatoes, bell peppers, corn, cucumbers, herbs, tomatoes, eggplant and others.

May arrived. As Scott and Elea were exiting the plant nursery and garden store located in the next town, Elea had a heart-to-heart talk with her friend as they stopped in the local luncheonette for a meal. She informed Scott of the conversation she had overheard on Easter Sunday morning when Beth and Avalene were standing outside of fellowship hall.

Scott said, "I don't know, Elea, Kyle might be a 'player'. If Beth is really telling the truth and he IS going to propose to her, and they'll co habitate together, I would keep my distance from both of them. Maybe the guy's a confused mess since he lost his wife."

Elea replied, "I'm always getting mixed signals from him, Scott. One minute I think he's really into me, the next I think he's still not over the loss of his wife. Then I get very confused whenever I see him with Beth and overhear her comments about him promising they'll get married."

Elea became deep in thought, "Listen, Scott, there's something else I didn't tell you."

Scott faced her with wide eyes. "And what's that?" he asked.

"No one knows about this. When I went to drop off a gift to Jack last Christmas night, Kyle and I sat and talked over glasses of wine in his living room. He told me the full story of how his wife passed and that he hadn't fully recovered from that loss. He explained how the pain still lingered. Close to the end of our discussion, he suddenly stopped speaking, inched over closer to me, stared into my eyes, and I knew for sure he was going to kiss me. As we were about ready to share a moment, I thought of Lane and how I shouldn't be in that situation. So I got up, said I needed to leave, grabbed my coat, and opened the door. He followed me as I stepped outside onto the porch. He stood behind me, put his arms around my waist, turned me around to face him, held me tight, and we both shared a long, passionate kiss. It was so hard for me to have not become caught up in that moment, but it happened. Then reality set in with regard to Lane. I broke loose of his arms and ran, saying I couldn't do this. When I fell back into the dorm that night, you must've noticed how unnerved I looked. I just felt so guilty for letting him kiss me like that. Throughout the train ride back to the city the following morning, I was feeling emotions I had never felt before."

Scott clearly remembered. "Wow, and you never told anyone about that?"

Elea replied, "Just my best friend Selene, from the city. She knows about it, and now so do you."

Scott responded, "This is a bit complex. It seems you have a guy in the city of whose relationship you're not sure. In this town there's a man whose body language is telling you he cares about you, isn't expressing his feelings, but hasn't committed to his current girlfriend. I suggest, my friend, that you just maintain your focus on this outreach ministry. Pray that God will enable the 'right' man to enter into your life one day. If things are meant to work out with either Lane or Kyle, you'll need to trust God to provide the answer." Scott's advice made good sense to her.

Elea responded, "Well, we're now into May, and our six-month extension will be over in August. Would you believe we've been here for close to a year already?

You're right, Scott, maybe I'm taking all of this stuff more seriously than I should be."

Scott smiled, as he put a comforting arm around Elea, "Let's go, girl, we've got a lot of planting and landscaping work ahead of us. And we really shouldn't forget the REAL purpose as to why we're all here. Just think, next year at this time, we'll be working in an altogether different community."

Elea smiled and nodded. As she and Scott drove back to the dorm, she reflected on her friend's sound words of advice and felt a sense of calm.

Judy S. Wagner

CHAPTER 15

THE SUMMER SEASON IN THE quaint laid-back town of Scarlet Oak Valley was a short one. After Sunday services, church members took advantage of the time to picnic, swim and fish in the local fresh-water lakes, go for countryside drives, visit in neighboring towns with friends and family, drink homemade lemonade, and savor delicious weekend dinners followed by homemade ice cream. They enjoyed the warmth of the sun as children played and rode bikes along dirt roads.

Scott, Elea and the volunteers never ceased working tirelessly among the youth and elderly communities throughout that summer season. The teen ministry organized various fundraisers and donated the proceeds to the homeless. The volunteers performed many other charitable works that benefitted both the church and local community.

The resurrection of a Vacation Bible School was planned for the last week of July. This was one of Elea's initiatives. She had the full support and cooperation of Reverend Ward and the church's senior deacons.

Reverend Ward requested that Elea meet with Beth beforehand with regard to scripture readings. The readings would be presented in the form of children's bible stories. It made sense to consult with Beth, as she was the coordinator of the church's weekly bible study group. Whenever Elea tried to contact Beth, despite leaving voicemails and other messages, Beth refused to return her calls.

Vacation Bible School week arrived. Partitions were set up in the fellowship hall, forming mini classrooms. Elea volunteered to take one of those classrooms, and discovered she had Jack as one of her students. Having never heard from Beth as to the scripture verses she should be presenting to her particular class, Elea referred to simple readings from the small Catholic bible she had in her possession.

When the class ended at noon on the first day of the program, Elea and Beth came face-to-face. Beth stood waiting for her outside of the classroom partition as the children exited her classroom.

Elea asked, "Beth, did you get my messages about the scripture material I'm supposed to present? I left quite a few messages on your answering machine, but never heard back from you."

"I never got any messages," Beth replied in a sarcastic tone, as she stood with her arms folded, glaring at Elea. She was obviously lying about never having been contacted. She added, "And what do you think you're doing reading to a 'Christian' group of children from a 'Catholic bible'? Reverend Ward will be furious when he finds out!"

Elea did her best to explain, "It was all I had in the form of materials, Beth. If it's not allowed, I apologize, but you never did return my calls. So I had to use whatever materials I could find."

Beth acted upset on purpose as she glared at Elea, "Well, don't, in fact, you shouldn't even BE a teacher in this program!" Having said that, she turned her nose up at Elea, and stalked away.

Elea sadly shook her head as she hopelessly watched Beth walk away annoyed. As she started to gather up her materials, she saw Jack standing silently observing.

"Hi, Jack," Elea smiled.

He responded, "I'm sorry she made you sad, Miss Elea. I really liked your class a lot, and all of the Bible stories you were telling us about." His adorable look of innocence totally captivated her.

"Thank you, sweetheart, you really added joy to my day." And with that, she stooped to tightly hug him.

The next day as Elea was ready to enter her classroom, she heard Kyle calling her name. She turned to face him.

"Elea, here, maybe you should use these materials for your class. I heard, Jack told me," he added, shaking his head, "I'm sorry she gave you such a hard time. So now you should be okay with using these." He tenderly smiled as he handed her the materials.

"Thanks," she replied, as she quietly smiled, and accepted them.

CHAPTER 16

THE SIX-MONTH EXTENSION WAS COMING to an end for Scott, Elea and the rest of the outreach volunteers. Reverend Ward requested one morning to meet with the two coordinators. When Scott and Elea entered the Reverend's office, additional chairs were set up, and they were very surprised to walk into an unexpected sea of faces.

"Come in, come in, Scott, Elea," spoke Reverend Ward, "Please take seats. I would like for both of you to meet some of the senior deacons of our church. Elea, I know you, Mrs. Ellison and Mrs. Grayson know one another quite well."

Elea smiled brightly, "Yes, hello Mrs. Ellison and Mrs. Grayson, hope you're both well." She hugged them, and then took a seat. Reverend Ward proceeded to introduce the other senior deacons who were in attendance.

"Our church's senior board of deacons has been discussing your outreach ministry. Once again, everyone feels you've been doing a magnificent job here. The board, including myself, would like to offer you one final six-month extension here to serve the underprivileged of Scarlet Oak Valley. If you don't mind, I've already spoken to your Father Bud. He said he had no issues with it. He added that he's delighted and is very proud of the job you're doing in our church and community. So once again, dear people, will you consider staying longer to help us?"

Scott and Elea glanced at everyone with surprise. The deacons all had radiant smiles on their faces and nodded as they stared at the two coordinators.

"This is such an honor, Reverend Ward. If all is good with Elea, we'll be most happy to continue with our work here."

Scott faced Elea and quietly asked, "Are you really okay with this?"

Elea nodded as she quietly responded, "I guess I'll have to be."

As they thanked Reverend Ward and the senior deacons and walked out the door, Elea thought, *Great, eighteen months will take us clearly into February. I know I won't be able to tolerate Beth showing off a diamond ring when she and Kyle get engaged this Christmas, or letting the world know they'll be living together. I'll need to leave this assignment before December arrives. Before Christmas, I'd like to be completely out of here.*

Elea kept those thoughts to herself. After having left Reverend Ward's office that morning, she was melancholy and was buried deep within her own thoughts. She took a long walk along the pleasant countryside road. When she returned to the dorm, she remained subdued for the remainder of that day.

"Hello, yes, Elea, you have a call," Scott said as he handed the phone to her. It was an early September evening.

"Hi, Rainy, how are you? It is SO good to hear from you! How's your sister in North Carolina doing? Reverend Ward read your letter to us. He said that she would need a lot of assistance, and that you were going to take care of her. He also said that you would be returning sometime in the future as the church's choir director."

Rainy replied, "Thank you for asking about Greta. She really hasn't been doing well these days, Elea. Actually, her cancer has spread, and the doctors are giving her two weeks at the max. They're discussing hospice care as the next step."

Rainy then held the phone away from herself, and Elea could hear her quiet sobs. "I'm so sorry, Rainy, we'll all pray for Greta and for you." Elea felt sad for her friend.

Rainy stopped sobbing and regained her composure, "Thank you, Elea. Listen, there's a possibility I may return to the church in the next couple of months, possibly by late November. I haven't communicated with Everett about any of this. I just need to get through everything with my sister first before making plans to settle back into Scarlet Oak Valley."

"Totally understandable, Rainy. I so miss you and wish you were back here, as I really could've used a good friend here at this church. A lot has happened since you traveled back to North Carolina last year." There was a moment of silence, as Elea could feel herself starting to become emotional.

Rainy spoke, "Oh, I think I understand what you're saying. It's Beth, isn't it? I guess she's really giving you a hard time, isn't she? That woman thinks she controls everything and everyone at that church, including Everett and Kyle. And it also doesn't help, Elea, that you're so pretty. I have no doubt she's very jealous of you."

Elea thanked Rainy and added, "I overheard Beth telling one of her friends that Kyle said he loved her. She said they would be getting engaged by this Christmas and that she would be living with Kyle and Jack, as well."

Rainy immediately exclaimed, "Are you kidding me? She's crazy if she thinks any of that is going to happen! I've known Kyle for a lot longer than she has. Trust me, while he may keep company with her and they date, I highly doubt he regards their relationship as more than just good friends. Listen, honey, we'll talk more when I see you. I have to run."

"Rainy, please know I'll be thinking of and praying for your dear sister and for you. Stay strong for Greta and keep me informed of everything, ok?" Elea responded.

Rainy was losing her voice again due to becoming emotional, and just replied, "I'll try my best, goodbye and thanks, Elea."

At the start of Sunday services in mid-September, there was a delay as the congregation impatiently sat and waited. Reverend Ward hadn't, as yet, entered the altar to conduct services that morning. Instead, Kyle, dressed in service vestments, approached the podium amidst looks of surprise from all of the church members. He looked breathtakingly handsome, yet intensely serious. He faced downward, looked up, then faced the congregation.

"Good morning." He took a breath, then continued, "Unfortunately, I have some devastating news to share with all of you. I regret to inform this congregation that our beloved pastor, the Reverend Doctor Everett Ward, passed away last night at the parsonage. Until a new pastor is determined, I'll be acting as your interim pastor. Let us all pray for God's mercy and forgiveness as we remember Dr. Ward in our prayers." And he solemnly led the congregation in prayer.

Scott reached over to hug Elea, who was clearly stunned and emotional upon hearing of the Reverend's sudden passing. They waited until after the prayer service to approach Kyle to express their condolences.

They offered their assistance, and that of the volunteers, with whatever help was needed.

All funeral arrangements were made by the church. At the burial service, when she was sure Elea noticed, Beth huddled into Kyle's arms as he hugged her with Jack standing alongside of them. Elea looked sad, closed her eyes, shook her head, and tried to concentrate on praying for the soul of the Reverend Doctor Ward.

The post-funeral luncheon followed the burial services for Reverend Ward. Elea continued on with her sadness throughout the day. She considered Reverend Ward's pleasant demeanor, kindness, support, and ever-constant faith in Scott, herself, and their volunteers. He was truly appreciative of everything the workers brought to the table and had every bit of confidence in all of them. She recalled his beautiful words and spirit of gratitude, and his encouragement of the church's senior deacons to continuously extend their assignment time.

The board of senior deacons met in October to determine a new pastor to head the small Evangelical Community Church. Unanimously, Kyle was voted in as the new pastor. By that time, he had finished his Doctor of Theology degree and was highly qualified to take on the responsible role of pastor. He moved into Reverend Ward's office. Beth conveniently made sure she promptly moved into Kyle's former office, thus using her small office as a cluttered file room.

CHAPTER 17

"**H**ELLO, RAINY! WHAT A NICE surprise, how are you?" Beth overheard Kyle's conversation, as he continued to speak, "Really! Well, I'm so sorry to hear about your sister, but thrilled you'll be returning here to take over the choirs! I, for one, have really missed not hearing your beautiful voice. Your hymn selections were the best, and the choir members always looked forward to the practices. I had taken on the role temporarily in your absence, and probably didn't do such a great job of it," he laughed. "And now with becoming the church's new pastor … . Oh, that's right, I guess you didn't hear. We lost Everett in mid-September, and the congregation's devastated! Yeah, it really was a shame, what a magnificent leader he was! Well, thank you. Yes, I finished up my Doctorate degree just as we learned the news of his passing. Okay, great, Rainy, hopefully, we'll meet up soon. So when again are you coming back to us? Alright, looking forward to seeing you. Bye."

Beth's immediate thoughts were, *Oh great, SHE'S coming back here!* In addition to her hatred for Elea,

Beth was also never fond of Rainy, and certainly didn't look forward to her return.

Kyle said as he smiled, "Beth, I have some good news. Rainy will be moving back to town by Thanksgiving and will be taking over the choirs. That'll be one huge task off of my plate. Actually, her return is great news for the church. Can you please note that I'll need to make the announcement at this Sunday's services?"

In response, Beth frowned and replied in a sarcastic tone, "Yup."

"Alright, Scott, let me go over and ask him if we can plan a 'Senior Day' and get the teen ministry involved. I'll be back in a few minutes," said Elea.

The volunteers had been discussing holding a "Senior Day" to honor the church's elderly members with a luncheon and some amateur entertainment from the teen ministry. An hour meeting would need to be called to discuss specifics. Elea suggested hosting the event a week prior to the Thanksgiving Day holiday. It was already the month of November.

From her office window, Beth noticed Elea walking in the direction of Kyle's office. Kyle was hard at work on his computer and was totally engrossed in church business. Beth strolled into his office and told him she suddenly felt dizzy, and asked that he please hold her before she might faint. He looked concerned for her, immediately got up from his desk, and complied.

Just as Elea approached his office and knocked softly on the half-opened door, Beth forced Kyle to kiss and hold her in a passionate embrace. She knew Elea was standing right outside his office door. She continued to press her lips hard against his. By the time Elea slowly opened the door, they were in full view.

Elea had seen enough. If she was never more convinced that Kyle was just a "player", she was totally convinced of it now. She quickly ran out of the church office and back into the dorm, trembling, near tears, and feeling very foolish.

"From what I just now saw, Scott, you're so right about Kyle being a 'player'". She explained to her fellow coordinator what had just taken place, "You go over and ask him if we could do a Senior Day. It's just too hurtful for me to interact with him, especially after what I just now saw."

When she knew Elea had run off, Beth eventually let loose of Kyle who was shocked by her sudden impulse.

"What was THAT all about, Beth? Why did you suddenly walk in here and force me to kiss you?" He stared at her in confused disbelief as he shook his head. He was clearly shaken.

A moment later, Scott knocked on the door. "Come in, Scott, Beth was just leaving," a somewhat embarrassed Kyle said, as he took hold of himself and welcomed Scott into his office.

"Was I interrupting something?" Scott gambled by asking the question.

"No, now what can I do for you?" Kyle responded, as Scott proceeded to discuss planning a "Senior Day" for the elderly members of the church.

Kyle replied, "Yes, of course, in fact, I've been meaning to meet with you and Elea to discuss future event planning. Let's have a meeting in the fellowship hall next Thursday night."

It was on a Sunday afternoon in November when Elea received a surprise phone call. "Lane....hi. I'm really surprised to hear from you."

Elea was genuinely shocked to hear from Lane, as they hadn't kept in touch since last Christmas. He never made any efforts to contact her during the spring season, as he had promised he would. She was convinced their relationship had been over for quite some time. He broke her heart by suggesting they date other people, and his body language proved he didn't care about her when they connected over the holiday break. So what could he possibly want?

"I really need to talk to you, Elea. When's the earliest I can see you?"

"Actually, Lane, I'm considering returning and settling back into Metro Line City before December. It's already November, so it will likely be sometime this month. I plan on talking to Scott, my fellow coordinator about my early departure. The team will be serving this community until next February, but my intentions are to leave here before Christmas." Elea's heart was breaking as she conveyed that information to Lane.

He responded, "That will work out great, and I can't wait to see you again, honey!" Elea held the phone away from her and shook her head, thinking *honey? Since when?*

Her head was spinning and she needed to ask, "Wait, Lane, what is up? Tell me, I want to know. Why are you contacting me all of a sudden when you made yourself abundantly clear last holiday season that you didn't want a serious commitment?"

"Ok, you got me", Lane conceded, "Since that last time, I did quite a bit of soul searching, and I really want for us to be a couple again. What I'm saying is no other people, just you and me."

Elea responded, "I need to clear my head, Lane. Wait until I return to Metro Line City. If you want to further discuss this when I return, we can. For now, I just want you to know that I'm not at all convinced of anything you're telling me. You showed in more ways than one how you didn't care about us or our relationship."

He replied, "Well, I hope you WILL consider it. Think back to our history and the great relationship bond we always shared. It was one that took us all the way back to our college days."

Elea replied, "I can't think straight right now. But I will call you when I arrive in Metro Line City. I've got to run." And with that said, Elea ended her call with Lane.

"You're not going to believe who just called me," Elea informed Scott. She added, "And I'll need to talk to you about my future plans with regard to remaining here in this town."

That Sunday night Scott sat, intently listening to everything Elea had explained to him. He hugged Elea, told her he understood her mixed emotions, yet wasn't going to inform anyone of her decision to return to Metro Line City that very month. She explained how she just wouldn't be able to cope with remaining in Scarlet Oak Valley throughout the holiday season. He said he wouldn't take formal steps to seek a replacement for her. He wanted to allow her time to re-think and reconsider her decision. He was devastated for Elea. Scott knew how much she really loved the outreach ministry and working among the poor and less fortunate in Scarlet Oak Valley.

Scott, Elea, Kyle and the volunteer workers, along with church members and the teen ministry, met the following Thursday night in the fellowship hall to discuss plans for a "Senior Day".

Elea was late in attending the one-hour meeting, contributed nothing in the way of suggestions, and looked sad and preoccupied throughout the ongoing discussions. She was half listening to the various members and volunteers putting forth some great suggestions, and half not paying attention. She seemed in a daze as she stared down at her notebook and wrote nothing.

Kyle was the first to notice. At the end of the meeting, Elea having not looked up once, nor spoken a word, stood and started to make her way out of the fellowship hall. Kyle was concerned and asked to speak to her alone.

"Elea, are you okay? You didn't say a word at the meeting tonight, and you didn't take notes. This isn't like you. What's going on?" He stood facing her with a look of confusion.

She took a breath, faced downward, and then faced Kyle, "This past Sunday, my boyfriend, or whoever he calls himself, phoned. I've known him since we first started to date in college. After graduation, we entered into a long-term relationship. I visited with him last holiday season and things didn't go well. He claimed he wasn't ready to commit to an exclusive relationship. He's apparently had quite a change of heart since then. The bottom line is that he told me he's now ready to seriously commit. I don't know what to think or say about it. Right now I feel like I'm taking a strange walk through the twilight zone."

Kyle looked stunned and he became serious. He faced her, and then asked, "How do YOU feel about him, Elea? Do you love him?"

She replied, "I thought there once was a time when I did. But now there's you, and with you and Beth getting engaged next month for Christmas...."

Kyle immediately interrupted her, "Whoa wait a minute. This is news to me. Since when, and where did you ever hear that rumor?"

Elea responded, "Beth was telling one of her friends last spring. I couldn't believe it at first, just from other 'messages' I was receiving from you. Then as I was on my way into your office last week, the two of you were kissing each other."

Kyle stood with his mouth open. It was at that moment when he realized Beth staged that whole "ready to faint" incident for the sake of Elea standing in full view of them.

Elea added, "Maybe it's me who should be asking if YOU love HER." She stared into his eyes, hoping so badly for the response she longed to hear. She hoped he would state that he really wanted to be with her and not with Beth.

Kyle, feeling insecure within himself, took a breath and tried to remain strong and unemotional. "Elea, from what my friend Brent explained to me last winter, I understand your boyfriend is a pretty successful guy. I heard he would be able to provide well for you and make a comfortable living where you'll have material goods and wealth all of your life. He's an investment broker, right? I understand they do very well financially."

He paused, then with reservations continued, "I think you really belong in the city, Elea, with a rich, successful man who could give you everything you want and which things you truly deserve."

He noticed the heartbroken look in her eyes, but felt compelled to add, "Brent also explained that you, yourself, said you missed the excitement of the city lights once you started your ministry here."

Elea stared into Kyle's eyes as tears started to form. "None of that materialism matters to me, Kyle. Since working as an outreach volunteer, I discovered a lot about myself and who I really am. I happen to love doing the Lord's work, especially among the poor and elderly. I don't need the city lights, a glamorous life, riches, or any of those non-important things, as much as I need a man who'll provide true love and an everlasting and unquestionable commitment."

Kyle, still concealing his true emotions, turned from Elea, then faced her and responded, "You weren't meant to be here, Elea. If your guy wants you back in the city, then go to him. You would never be happy here. This poor town isn't good enough for someone like you who's used to so much better."

She heard enough. She was thoroughly convinced Kyle had absolutely no feelings for her, despite that one-time kiss. At that moment it dawned on her how she had totally taken out of context the times he would stare lovingly into her eyes and act as if he wanted to say so much more to her. Now she knew how he REALLY felt about her. Maybe he was just a "player" after all.

As Kyle stood facing downward, Elea quickly ran out of the fellowship hall, with tears streaming down her face. He looked back up, watched her run, and felt helpless. He instantly regretted having spoken the uncaring words to her that he did. Yet, confusion was running rampant in his mind. He'd been questioning himself all along as to whether he would really be able to commit to Elea. Would he be able to provide her with a lifetime of happiness, considering that he was just a full-time pastor of a poor southern community church?

She had made herself perfectly clear to him, yet he questioned if her happiness with him would only be temporary. After all, she was used to so much more in the way of material things, thanks to a rich, successful boyfriend. Would she miss all of that and ultimately become regretful that she hadn't married her wealthy college man?

After Jack had gone to bed that night, Kyle sat deep in thought over the emotional discussion he and Elea had that day. He felt very regretful. He considered the heartbroken look in her eyes as he foolishly spoke the cold, uncaring words to her that he did.

Why couldn't I tell her how I REALLY felt about her? She said she could be happy here. How could I have been so foolish as to not have expressed my true feelings to her when it was obvious it was what she had hoped to hear?

CHAPTER 18

THE WEEK BEFORE THE THANKSGIVING Day holiday, Elea briefly stopped into the fellowship hall. She paused to observe and enjoy a few minutes of the Senior Day luncheon and the entertainment provided by the teen ministry. She was grateful Kyle was not physically present at the event, as he was busy working in his office. He was the last person she wanted to see.

Elea said goodbye to all of the volunteers, and quickly and privately planned her exit out of Scarlet Oak Valley, Tennessee. One of the volunteers would be driving her to the local train station. Prior to departing, Elea had contacted her Metro Line City best friend Selene. She informed her of what had happened with Kyle, and that she would be permanently returning to the city. She had asked Selene if she could remain at her apartment until she could find a place of her own. Elea offered to share the cost of the rent with her friend, but Selene declined to accept any kind of reimbursement. Selene added, "For reasons which I'll explain when we meet up in person." First on Elea's agenda, however, would be to connect with Lane when she returned.

"Oh, Scott, can you please give this letter to Rainy once she arrives. It's got all of my contact information in it. And please tell her I love her and hope to hear from her." Scott sadly nodded as he took the letter from Elea and put it on the countertop.

She added, "Maybe it's better you don't inform Mrs. Ellison and the seniors as to the real reason why I'm leaving. Just tell them that a family emergency came up and I don't know for how long I'll be gone. By the time February arrives, it won't matter anyway, so let them all think I'll be returning soon."

Scott sadly nodded once again, and replied, "Give me a hug, girlfriend, and please stay in touch. Remember, you're welcome back here anytime. We're not filling your spot, and I'm not saying a word to Father Bud about this. And listen, if I don't see you by Christmas, have a happy!" Scott added, as he tightly hugged Elea. Their friendship was a solid one.

Elea boarded the train that morning and began her journey back to Metro Line City. She sadly considered her entire experience in Scarlet Oak Valley. *It's probably for the best. He made it abundantly clear he was never in love with me. I'll head back to the city, look for an apartment, and apply for work at one of the schools. I'll use my degree there as I once did before I became involved in this outreach ministry.*

Rainy had returned to the small community church by Thanksgiving weekend, as planned. She barely missed connecting with Elea.

As she made her way into the church office, Kyle looked up from his desk and warmly greeted her. "Rainy, welcome back! Listen, I think I would like for you to take over Beth's former office. She's taken over my office, I've taken over Everett's, and all that's left is the empty office filled with old files and the copier. The clutter needs to be removed from that room. You've been looking for office space for a while now, so please make plans to have someone help you clear it out so you can use it. It would also be better so that you and I can communicate without me having to call you throughout the course of the day." Rainy seemed pleased, nodded, and thanked Kyle.

Just then, Scott knocked on the door to Kyle's office where Kyle and Rainy were in discussion. Scott had stopped in to see Kyle that morning and to explain Elea's sudden departure. As she requested, Scott used the excuse that she needed to leave due to a family emergency. Scott also explained that as far as he knew, Elea would be returning soon.

"Ah, Rainy, hello, it's so great to see you again!" Scott smiled and enthusiastically hugged the former choir director. He added, "Please accept all of the volunteers', as well as my own condolences over the passing of your sister, Greta." Rainy sadly nodded and thanked him.

Scott added, "I thought I saw you walking in this direction, so I ran back to the dorm to grab this letter and give it to you. It's from Elea." After handing her the letter, he smiled and left the office.

Rainy took a seat in Kyle's office and started to silently read the contents of Elea's letter. She noticed Kyle seemed interested in its contents, as well.

After reading, she looked up, faced him and said, "Well, Elea's out of here. She took the train back to Metro Line City and said here in her letter that she doesn't plan on ever returning. She did, however, leave me with her contact information."

Rainy continued, "She was wonderful, Kyle, and I'm really upset she's gone, but I'll definitely stay in touch with her." With that said, Rainy left Kyle's office to check out her new office space.

Kyle became very sad after Rainy revealed that Elea's intentions were not to return to Scarlet Oak Valley. That certainly wasn't what Scott explained when he spoke to him earlier that day. He knew Elea was upset when they last spoke, yet he was surprised that she actually moved forward as quickly as she did with heading back to Metro Line City. This would be a permanent move for her. He would never see her again. Shocked by the realization, regrets instantly set in.

Kyle tapped on the door to Rainy's office, "You said Elea left her contact information. May I have it?" His concern clearly showed.

Rainy smiled, "Sure, give me a minute to write it down for you."

Kyle couldn't stop thinking of Elea throughout the day, the evening, and especially when he was alone. He knew he should wait no longer to finally tell her how he really felt about her, and could think of nothing else. His determination at that moment was to follow her to Metro Line City and try to win her back.

"Hey bud, how would you like to take an early Christmas trip with me to Metro Line City? We'll surprise Miss Elea with a visit, but we won't say anything to anyone, ok?"

Kyle smiled as he observed the radiant look on Jack's face.

"Yes, daddy, can we go? I can't wait to see Miss Elea again!"

Kyle was thrilled his son was so excited, and responded with great enthusiasm to his suggestion.

The weekend after Thanksgiving, leading into early December, Kyle and Jack boarded the train after Sunday services. They headed to one of New York's busiest metropolises. They both looked so handsome in their dress pants, shirts and jackets as they arrived and checked into a local hotel.

"We'll enjoy a great dinner tonight, Jack, and then tomorrow we'll surprise Miss Elea with a visit." Kyle told his son, who was anxiously looking forward to it.

Kyle called for a cab and asked the driver which restaurant he would recommend he and his son patronize for dinner, as they weren't familiar with any of the bistros in the city. Kyle intended to question Jack during dinner regarding his feelings about Elea, along with the possibility that he was considering professing his love to her.

His friend Brent Somerville's words kept resonating in his head, *If you have feelings for that beautiful woman, I would suggest you let her know. Otherwise, someone else will scoop her up before you've had that opportunity, and then you will have lost her.* Kyle was convinced that was exactly what he should do.

Once inside the exclusive-looking bistro recommended by the cab driver, the waiter seated Kyle and Jack and handed them their menus. As part of a Christmas gift to Jack, Kyle had enough money set aside to treat his son to a great meal in a pricey restaurant. He scanned the inside of the venue, in awe of its expensive-looking décor. At that moment, his eyes immediately spotted Elea and Lane. They were sitting enjoying a cozy dinner by the fireplace on the opposite side of the room. His heart raced the minute he saw her.

There she was, looking both beautiful and desirable. She was wearing an elegant evening dress adorned with exquisite diamond accessories. They were obviously tokens of affection provided to her by her wealthy guy. It was evident how her handsome boyfriend was showering her with compliments. Lane hadn't taken his eyes off of her for a minute. Elea was smiling and looking happy and comfortable in her element. Kyle, in the meantime, hadn't stopped staring in their direction, slowly drinking everything in, while dying on the inside.

Then appeared before his eyes his worst nightmare. With a look of total surprise on Elea's face, he saw Lane get down on one knee. He took hold of her hand as he was speaking to her, and offered her a diamond ring!

Kyle couldn't bear to remain in the restaurant another minute! He threw down his menu and grabbed his son by the hand, never casting a backward glance as to whether or not Elea accepted Lane's proposal. He quickly exited the restaurant with Jack. In his mind, she most likely would accept Lane's proposal, and he would never be able to bear the thought of Elea and Lane wrapped in each other's arms and sharing love. Meanwhile, Jack was oblivious to everything.

"Jack, I'm sorry, son, let me get you some dinner from somewhere. I'm not feeling very well and we need to leave the city. I'll check out the train schedule and get us back to Scarlet Oak Valley as soon as possible."

Jack was confused and asked, "We're not going to surprise Miss Elea with a visit, dad?"

Kyle was sad, glanced downward, then faced Jack, "No, son, I'm sorry, we won't be seeing Miss Elea anymore." Jack looked disappointed.

Throughout the long train ride back to Scarlet Oak Valley, Kyle just gazed out of the window, shaken and feeling defeated by that heartbreaking restaurant incident. When he returned to his church office on Monday morning, he was noticeably sad and preoccupied throughout that entire week, barely interacting with anyone. His mind and heart were consumed with Elea. Now it was entirely too late to make himself known to her. He should've acted when he still had the chance. He envisioned her and Lane being happy together, yet kept hoping in the back of his mind that she hadn't accepted his marriage proposal. Though the prospects appeared dim, he hoped there might exist the possibility that Elea would still have feelings for him.

After much soul searching and quiet walks down dusty country roads in solitude, Kyle prayed and ultimately resigned himself to the fact that he would never see Elea again. He was certain that his dreams had ended that she would one day become his wife and be a great stepmother to Jack. Lane was obviously the right man for her.

He continued to struggle with his feelings, *Who am I kidding? She's made her choice. He can clearly give her what she deserves. She has no real future with me. I could never provide for her in the way that he can. She's used to nice things and the excitement of the city environment. She'll have all of that with him. I love her and only want*

what's best for her, but the question now is how do I deal
with my broken heart?

"Hi Rainy, can I see you in my office?" Rainy had just
finished Friday afternoon's practice sessions with the
Christmas choirs. Kyle deliberately sent Beth back to
his house to care for Jack. He really needed some alone
time with Rainy.

"Yes, Pastor Williams, what can I do for you?" a
smiling Rainy responded as she entered Kyle's office
and took a seat. Kyle looked up from his desk, ran his
hand through his hair, then sat back.

He spoke, "You and I have always been good friends,
and you tell me you and Elea have also become good
friends. I feel I need to talk to someone and would
certainly appreciate your hearing me out on this."

"Of course, Kyle, anytime," responded Rainy, as she
saw the look of concern on his face. She ventured to
ask, "By the way, have you been upset about anything
in particular this past week?"

He faced downward, nodded, looked back up and
replied, "Yes, this is why I felt I needed to talk to you.
At first I couldn't believe it when Scott stopped in,
asking if he could explain to me why Elea suddenly
headed back to Metro Line City. He explained she had
some sort of 'family emergency' going on at home, and
that she would be back soon. Luckily, our congregation

believed it when I announced it at services last Sunday. Many of our members asked specifically when she would return. Then Scott returned to my office to hand you Elea's letter when he noticed you were here. I'm pretty sure I know exactly why she left. Elea probably wrote to you about why she's no longer here, didn't she?" Rainy sat listening to Kyle, sighed as she faced downward, then nodded.

In her private letter to Rainy, Elea explained all she had been through with Kyle. She emphasized the hatred and resentment she had constantly endured with Beth. She emphasized her rudeness, the comments and criticisms she always faced from her, and the devastating announcement she "happened" to overhear about Kyle being in love with her. Elea stood motionless as she overheard Beth tell Avalene that Kyle intended to propose to her at Christmas time. She also informed Rainy of the kiss Kyle and Beth shared, which she was conveniently meant to see.

In her letter, Elea confided to Rainy how she believed Kyle was feeling about her the same as she was feeling about him. She noted how those feelings surfaced at various times. She informed Rainy of the passionate way he kissed her on his front porch last Christmas night, and the reason why she needed to run from him.

Her final words to Rainy explained her discussion with Kyle prior to Thanksgiving, and how she fully realized it wasn't what she thought it was. She informed Rainy of how her heart ached when he actually suggested she head to Metro Line City to be with Lane. She explained how Kyle had the perfect opportunity at that moment to express his feelings for her. His overall demeanor, lack of emotions and uncaring words, broke her heart. She was devastated that he really hadn't fought for her. Since Elea's letter to Rainy was confidential, Rainy didn't discuss its contents with Kyle, except for when he asked for her contact information.

Kyle explained to Rainy the purpose of why he had taken Jack into Metro Line City on the Sunday after Thanksgiving. He also informed her of what he had observed in the restaurant where he spotted Elea and Lane.

Rainy questioned, "Kyle, from what you had witnessed at the restaurant that evening, are you SURE Elea accepted her boyfriend's proposal? You claimed you grabbed Jack and just ran out of there without knowing for sure."

He replied, "From what I had seen, I would've assumed she did. I just couldn't last another minute observing all of it that night. She looked so beautiful and they looked so perfect together. It really put me over the edge."

Rainy responded, "From how I understood it, Kyle, didn't you pretty much influence Elea's decision to head back to the city? She and I always kept in touch. I know she was so heartbroken when you showed her you didn't care. It appeared you encouraged her to resume her former relationship with Lane. In addition, there was this business of you and Beth planning on getting engaged by Christmas."

Kyle sat back, frowned, and adamantly stated, "I don't plan on asking Beth to marry me, Rainy. And I don't appreciate her telling her friends and others that it's even going to happen."

Rainy explained, "From outward appearances, Kyle, you and Beth are always seen together. Members of this congregation are convinced at this point that you two have been a couple for three years now. And usually, the relationship progresses forward. I can't blame Elea for being upset when she walked in on you and Beth kissing each other. What else was she supposed to think?"

Kyle took a deep breath and nodded. He explained to Rainy how he believed Beth may have staged that incident, and that he had no intentions of kissing her. He and Rainy continued their heartfelt discussion throughout the early evening.

In Metro Line City, Elea was also sad and pre-occupied throughout that week. Her response to Lane at the restaurant that evening was that she would thoroughly need to think things through before committing to his proposal. She and Lane never became engaged the night when Kyle had spotted them. However, Lane did agreed to provide Elea with a little more time to consider his proposal. He adamantly stated that he refused to be kept waiting long. He was on the verge of relocating to the west coast and needed her response.

Elea spoke at length with her best friend, Selene, about everything that had happened in Scarlet Oak Valley. She had a final decision to make as to whether or not to accept Lane's proposal. There was a time she dreamed of that special moment when Lane would ask for her hand in marriage. Never did she imagine that she would fall in love with another man, but a man, unfortunately who didn't feel the same way about her. She couldn't get Kyle out of her mind. He only complicated her decision about whether or not she should become engaged to Lane.

Judy S. Wagner

CHAPTER 19

"SELENE, I NEED TO BE honest with Lane. We're supposed to have dinner tomorrow night, and he's really pressing me for my response to his marriage proposal. Even though Kyle has no interest in me, I'm not in love with Lane and need to be honest with him. He wants an answer before he leaves the city in a couple of days and permanently relocates to the west coast."

"Speaking of relocating, Elea, I have some news of my own to share, girlfriend," Selene excitedly exclaimed. She and Elea were eating dinner in the apartment that night.

Elea faced her friend with wide eyes. "So tell me, Selene, what's going on?"

Selene explained, "I met someone during last year's ski trip to Vermont. At first he was acting really shy and wasn't contacting me. But as these months moved on, I started hearing from him a lot. We made plans to meet up and have been hitting it off so well. Bottom line is that when this apartment lease expires at the end of this year, I don't plan on renewing it. Instead, I'll be relocating to Ohio, in the same town where Ian lives."

"I'm so happy for you, Selene," excitedly replied Elea, as she smiled warmly at her friend. Elea was genuinely happy for Selene.

"I wanted to ask, Elea, if you would like to take over the lease once I'm gone."

Elea thought about it for a few seconds, then responded, "That's sweet of you to think of me, Selene. This space is great and I've appreciated that you've accommodated my visits. For myself, though, I would look for a smaller apartment. Thanks for the heads up. What I'll do now is contact area rental agencies to see what places may be available. Since I started with the outreach ministry, maintaining an apartment would have been a waste, considering we volunteers travel from location to location with our aero beds. But now since deciding to move back here permanently, I'll need to consider options. The timing will work out well, since you'll be vacating this apartment in another month. The rental agency, I'm sure, will have found me something to my liking by then. For now, I'm just so grateful you're allowing me to stay here."

Selene smiled and nodded. Elea then toasted to Selene's great news! She hugged and wished her friend all the best.

The next evening over dinner, Elea ended her relationship with Lane. She refused his marriage proposal. She also found herself confiding to him everything that had happened throughout her ministry in Scarlet Oak Valley. She even spoke about Kyle.

Lane sat attentively listening to her with a look of bewilderment on his face. He shook his head and asked, "So why would you ever want to be in a relationship with an older guy who's been married, struggles financially, and has a kid? Don't you think you deserve better than what HE can provide for you, Elea? With me, you'll have everything, a spacious home, expensive cars, we could travel, and you could buy anything you want. If you want to work, you can. If not, then you can afford to stay at home and have a nanny help you with the kids. I can give you all of that, and more. I'm very confused as to why you would choose to 'settle'?"

"Yes, Lane, it's true, you can certainly afford to provide me with the world, but maybe you're overlooking the most important point: That I may not be looking for the same thing. Maybe I don't care if my husband can't afford to provide for me as well, financially, as you could. I obtained a teaching degree and taught at one time, so I could always fall back on that. I also have a graduate degree in social work. It's what I was doing before I started my ministry in Scarlet Oak Valley. I've always had a calling to help less fortunate people, and so much help is needed in many underprivileged areas throughout the U.S."

Elea explained, "For the first time in my life, I felt a sense of 'gratification' I had never felt before, and was so confident I was where I was meant to be. There was a time when I would've never traded the glamour, bright lights and excitement of Metro Line City. When you and I were together and I was so sure of your love, I looked forward to experiencing more of that with you. But my entire perspective has changed since our discussion last year."

Elea continued, "Please understand you and I have nothing more in common now, Lane. You want one thing out of life; I want something else, something that far surpasses wealth. I want the joy of working within a less fortunate community of beautiful, underprivileged people. These are poor people whose faces brighten whenever they look into your face and are so grateful for any help you can give them. It's the greatest sense of love and fulfillment one could ever dream possible. I know it's very hard for someone like you to understand, especially if you haven't experienced it."

"Well, if that's what you're really looking for, Elea, and you're right, I just don't understand it. Personally, I have no desire to, either. But if that's what you really want, then go for it." Lane responded, as he frowned and shook his head.

Following dinner and his marriage proposal having been refused, Lane dropped Elea back off to Selene's apartment. He walked her upstairs, gave her a hug and kiss and said, "I wish you the best of everything, Elea." As he was heading toward the elevator area, he called her name and she turned to face him, "He's a pretty lucky man."

With a melancholy look on her face, she stood staring as Lane entered through the elevator doors and permanently walked out of her life.

"I said no to him, Rainy. Lane and I will not be getting married," Elea explained to her friend one night as they spoke.

Rainy wasn't surprised and replied, "Elea, I really wish you would come back to Scarlet Oak Valley to resume working with our community. The world misses you and has been upset ever since you left!"

"That's so sweet of you to say, Rainy, I know, even Scott's encouraging me to return every time I've spoken with him. But how could I possibly do that? I just can't, knowing Kyle and Beth will soon get engaged, and especially knowing how I still feel about him."

Rainy responded, "That's another something else we need to discuss, Elea."

Rainy knocked on the door to Kyle's office. He looked up. "Just thought you should know she said no to him." That having been said, Rainy smiled, quietly closed the door behind her, and settled herself into her new office. Kyle looked up surprised, stopped working on his Sunday sermon, and sat back for a few minutes in deep thought.

A few minutes later, Beth entered his office and locked the door behind her. She faced Kyle. "So, I was hoping to talk to you about us. Are we getting engaged in another week, or what, Kyle? Christmas is coming up."

He stared at her, surprised and confused. "Whatever are you talking about, Beth? And I heard you've been announcing to your friends that I'm in love with you and that we'll be getting engaged by Christmas. I heard you're also telling your friends you and I will be living together. I mean, I'm fond of you and appreciate the way you help out with Jack, but you may be seeing our relationship very differently than what it really is."

Beth boldly took a seat on his lap, put her arms around his neck, and started to kiss him. Kyle was clearly uncomfortable and insisted she stop. "I'm so glad SHE'S not here anymore." He realized Beth was referring to Elea. She whispered in his ear, "I just wish you would quit dragging your feet, Kyle. You know you love me and want for you, Jack and myself to be a family, so I don't get why you're not proposing."

Kyle immediately released himself from Beth's grip, stood up, stared into her face, and coldly replied, "I really think you should resign your position with this church, Beth. The reality of it all is that I am NOT in love with you and never will be, so please stop trying to convince yourself there's love between us when you know that's not true!" He was very annoyed.

Beth was livid and screamed, "That does it, I'm out of here, buddy. I'll be leaving on the fastest train out of this insane, pathetic town of losers you call 'home'. And thanks for totally wasting my time for these past three years!" With that said, she gave him a hard shove, enabling him to fall back against his desk, and ran out the door, slamming it shut behind her.

Rainy overheard a good deal of the drama. She opened her office door, poked her head out, and when the coast was clear, walked over to Kyle's office. She allowed a few minutes for him to take a breath and settle down, then asked, "Are you okay, pastor?"

Kyle, still a bit shaken, nodded, then explained, "Beth's leaving town, Rainy. I suggested she resign her position with the church. Listen, it may be a bit too soon to ask, but how would you like to assume the role of my church assistant? You can relocate into my former office first thing tomorrow morning. Do you think you'd be able to work with me during normal business hours, in addition to coordinating both choirs on Wednesday evenings? I can take over the Wednesday night bible study."

A real sense of relief came over Rainy, "Absolutely, boss, and it would be MY honor to take on both of those roles!" She and Kyle embraced each other, smiling.

As they both turned to go back into their offices, he called her name and she turned to face him. He smiled and spoke, "Oh, and I did hear what you said earlier about 'her' saying no to 'his' proposal."

Rainy could hardly contain her excitement! She immediately reached out to Elea to inform her of the falling out between Kyle and Beth, as well as Beth's plans to permanently leave Scarlet Oak Valley.

Rainy excitedly said, "Just wanted to let you know Kyle's a single man again. Elea, I really wish you would consider returning to our community. Everyone here loves you and is always asking when you're coming back. 'Family emergencies' can only be used as excuses for just so long. Kyle cares about you, sweetheart, I know that for a fact."

As Elea strolled the cold, blustering sidewalks of Metro Line City, she stopped for a hot cup of coffee in one of the cafes. She took the time to reflect on her recent conversations with both Scott and Rainy. Should she give it another try and return to Scarlet Oak Valley, a place she had grown so fond of and really missed since the day she hastily departed from there?

She booked a ticket and intended to visit the quaint town on Christmas Day. She informed Scott and Rainy

of her plans, asking they not let anyone else know. Both
of them were looking forward to seeing her.

Judy S. Wagner

CHAPTER 20

I T WAS ON CHRISTMAS DAY when Elea arrived in Scarlet Oak Valley. That holiday morning, Kyle was preaching a profound Christmas message to his congregation. He momentarily paused as he spotted Elea opening the front doors of the church, quietly taking a seat in the last row. A social hour followed services. Kyle, still looking breathtakingly handsome in his service vestments, along with Jack, proceeded downstairs to the fellowship hall. Both were very surprised and happy to see her.

"What a surprise! Merry Christmas, Elea, you look beautiful!" Kyle said, with a mesmerized look on his face, as he reached out to hug her.

"Thanks, Merry Christmas, Kyle and Jack," she smiled and stooped to give Jack a big hug. Jack was thrilled to see her!

"Daddy, can we ask Miss Elea to come for Christmas dinner at our house today?"

Kyle smiled, as he patted his son on the head, "Absolutely, if Miss Elea hasn't made other plans."

She smiled and responded, "I would love to. Just let me know what time dinner is ready and what you need."

Kyle lovingly gazed at her, smiled and said, "Great, see you then at 6:00 p.m. and no need for you to bring anything. Jack and I will have it all covered."

Elea was warmly received by the entire congregation. She happily smiled, greeted, and fellowshipped with everyone in the church hall. Even Beth's clique of women friends smiled and wished her a Merry Christmas. Avalene even hugged and welcomed her, and they chatted for a few minutes.

"Rainy!" exclaimed Elea, as she walked over to hug and greet her friend.

"Are you back? I surely hope so!" exclaimed an excited Rainy. "These folks have really missed you, Elea. We're always hearing from one member or another how much they wished you were still here!"

Elea explained, "I guess I'll know soon, Rainy, if returning back here was a good idea. Just so you know, our volunteers have two final months left here in Scarlet Oak Valley. Father Bud informed Scott that our eighteen-month time couldn't be extended any further, and that we would have to move on to another underprivileged community. So in any event, we'll all be forced to leave this town by the end of February."

Rainy was very disappointed, "Oh, that's too bad! Even if Kyle discusses with Father Bud that our community, especially the elderly, still need a lot of help, will that make a difference?"

Elea explained, "No, I'm afraid not, Rainy. The Catholic Volunteers organization we were told has been through this scenario many times in the past working with other communities. The problem is that folks become too attached, in the hopes the volunteers will remain in their communities indefinitely. Our mission in serving these underprivileged communities is to educate the people, in order to help them grow and be able to help themselves. Once they're equipped with the necessary tools, the hope would be that they would be able to continue that process and improve their lives. So we were told up front that we weren't allowed to remain in any one place beyond the eighteen months."

Rainy sadly nodded. The two friends once again embraced and sat down to enjoy coffee and Christmas cookies and to catch up with each other.

It was early evening when Elea made her way over to Kyle's house from the dorm. The small country home looked quite festive on the inside, with a tall, beautiful evergreen tree decorated with lights and garland. Clear single-bulb candles graced each window of the house, adding to a calm and peaceful environment.

She was served a dinner of roast beef, mashed potatoes and green beans that both Kyle and Jack made, utilizing whatever basic cooking skills they had acquired. The meal was simple and delicious. It was late that evening, Jack had already gone to bed, Kyle poured Elea some wine and they sat and talked.

"Where do I begin?" Kyle initiated the discussion, as he smiled and sat comfortably next to Elea, "I assume Rainy kept you up to speed on things here at the church, how Beth left our community, and how Rainy is now the church assistant and heads both choirs. And you already knew I was confirmed as pastor."

Elea responded, "Yes, she did. I'm excited for Rainy, and I have no doubt this church will thrive under your wonderful leadership, Kyle."

He then became subdued, and with a look of concern on his face said, "We should talk, Elea, I'll get straight to the point. I heard you didn't accept Lane's marriage proposal. I guess I'm confused as to why you didn't. I mean, look at you, you're so beautiful and desirable! When Jack and I spotted you and Lane in the restaurant that one night we took a trip to surprise you, you couldn't have looked any more gorgeous. Everyone there was staring at what a great looking couple you and Lane made. And you both looked so happy. You have no idea that night how I wished so badly I could've been THAT guy." He sadly looked down as he sipped his wine.

Elea stated, "I didn't accept his proposal, Kyle, and for one reason only – I'm NOT in love with Lane. If YOU had approached our table that night, I know I would've left the restaurant with you and Jack, and would've returned to Scarlet Oak Valley with both of you."

He continued to stare into her eyes. Kyle apparently was still feeling insecure and having mixed emotions regarding Elea. He still questioned whether or not he could provide Elea with a comfortable life, a life which excluded all of the material things she'd been used to with Lane. He kept stressing that point to her.

"Kyle, none of what Lane could provide for me could ever compare to true love, God, church and community. Those are MY priorities and not Lane's."

"Do you really believe you could be happy with me, Elea?" Kyle asked.

"I know I can be, Kyle," Elea responded, as she got up from the sofa. He also stood. He stared into her eyes, pulled her tightly into a loving embrace, and started to passionately kiss her.

But then he suddenly broke loose, and shook his head saying, "No, even though I love you so much, I can never give you what you've been used to. Maybe in the beginning you would be happy, but ultimately you would regret being the wife of just a small town, full-time church pastor who struggles to make ends meet."

Elea became emotional, "You're missing the point, Kyle, as long as we both love each other, we'd be able to get through anything. I can't emphasize enough that I don't need what you're claiming I do. Lane offered the world and I said no. My true love and passion is to work and grow within this precious community, and the hell with everything else!"

With tears in her eyes she added, "But I'm SO tired of trying to convince you of that!" Shaking her head and feeling totally defeated, she grabbed her coat and ran out the door crying. Kyle called after her, but she didn't look back.

She returned to the dorm devastated. Scott immediately noticed how upset she was. Elea informed him that she would be leaving Scarlet Oak Valley, never to return, first thing in the morning on the earliest train out of the city. No other trains were scheduled to leave town that evening, so she was forced to remain in the town until early dawn.

"Do let Father Bud know this time, Scott, that I won't ever return to this outreach ministry, not here and not anywhere else. It's been way too heartbreaking of an experience to continue doing this. What if I meet another Kyle along the way?"

The phone in the dorm rang. Scott answered it, got Elea's attention, and whispered, "Kyle wants to see you."

Elea responded, "Well, I don't ever want to see him."

Scott continued, "I'm sorry, Kyle."

"He heard your background response," Scott told Elea, "He said he couldn't leave Jack alone in the house sleeping, but that he would stop here first thing tomorrow morning to talk to you."

Elea angrily responded, "Well, that's too bad for him now, isn't it? I'll be out of here at the crack of dawn on the earliest train headed back to Metro Line City." It was obvious she intended to stand by her decision.

She sobbed as she continued speaking, "Scott, can you please give this small gift to Jack for me? I forgot to bring it with me tonight at dinner, and also tell him I'll always love him."

Early dawn the following morning, Elea asked one of the volunteers to drive her to the local train station. The fresh, early-morning air was frigid, and the train station was dark and deserted.

Just as Elea was ready to board the train, still very much upset, she thought she heard both Kyle and Jack calling her name. She turned around. Both were out of breath as they eventually reached where she was standing.

Kyle tightly took hold of her arms as he stared into her eyes, "Don't leave. Remember when you said you would pray that God would one day send an angel into our lives? Well, you ARE that angel, Elea. I've never been more certain of that."

She broke loose of his grip, shook her head and responded, "No, that special angel will enter your lives one day, and you'll be convinced from the start when that happens. You won't need to second guess yourself, as you'll be sure. And you were never sure of us, Kyle." The train doors opened and she was ready to step in.

Kyle pleaded, "Please don't leave us, Elea, Jack and I both love you so much! Stay and make our church home your home." She turned away from him, trying her best to ignore his words.

He refused to let her step into the train, grabbed hold of her arms and pulled her close to him.

"No Kyle..." He didn't want to hear anything more. He held her tight and passionately kissed her, resisting her efforts to break loose, until she finally succumbed to his lips and strong, unrelenting embrace.

"I love you, Elea," he said as he continued kissing her and staring into her tear-filled eyes, "I always have, but I was too insecure and foolish thinking I was never good enough for you. I know you love everyone in our community and totally believe that nothing else matters to you, except your passion and desire to help others. Your 'home' is here with us."

Kyle, Elea and Jack all hugged one another tightly. Elea stooped to give Jack a big hug and kiss of his own, while Kyle stood proudly. Jack never looked happier in his life as he glanced upward at his dad and Elea and radiantly smiled.

That same morning when Elea returned to the dorm, all of the volunteers, and especially Scott, were shocked and thrilled to welcome her back.

"What? I mean Why? How?" Scott questioned, as he shook his head in total amazement! He certainly hadn't expected to ever see Elea again.

"I'm so thrilled, but what are you doing back here?" he asked, wide-eyed with the same look of amazement on his face.

Elea excitedly replied, "Kyle and Jack held me back from stepping into the train. Kyle professed his love and insisted on taking me back to Scarlet Oak Valley."

Scott was elated and happily responded, "Well, I'm so glad the guy finally stepped up! And I never did make that call to Father Bud about you," he added with a wink.

Elea beamed, "I'm so glad you didn't, because I'm back again and so ready to work for the last two months we'll all be here."

Scott replied, "Lady, I have a feeling you'll never be leaving this town."

Elea also phoned Selene to inform her of the change of plans. She explained that she would remain in Scarlet Oak Valley with Scott and the rest of the volunteers. Elea explained to Selene how Kyle professed his love for her at the train station. Selene was ecstatic and conveyed her best wishes of love and future happiness to her friend.

The Christmas holiday season turned out to be warm and joyous for everyone that year. Kyle planned a visit to his parents' home in Arkansas right before the New Year. He wanted to introduce Elea to his parents and family. His parents, siblings and relatives all adored Elea after having met and spoken to her. Everyone showed their overwhelming love and support when Kyle announced to them that he had serious intentions with regard to Elea. Everyone couldn't have been more thrilled for Kyle and Jack, as they all welcomed Elea with open arms.

CHAPTER 21

T HE MONTH OF FEBRUARY ARRIVED, and Valentine's Day that year fell on a Sunday. After services, Kyle called a meeting with the entire congregation. He stepped up to the podium in fellowship hall to address everyone.

"Please know our congregation has deeply appreciated the hard work and time-consuming efforts of these incredible volunteers. They've accomplished so much for our church and community for these past eighteen months. Due to their assignment restrictions, I'm very sad to announce they'll need to move on to their next six-month 'tour of duty' at the end of this month. However, they'll still be with us for two more weeks. The next church and community who welcomes these wonderful people should consider themselves incredibly blessed; I know we certainly have been."

Kyle continued, "My message this morning comes as a mixed bag of blessings. While Scott Preston and the volunteers will need to move on, I'm refusing to allow one of these volunteers to leave us." At that moment, he faced Elea and smiled. He then moved from the podium over to where she stood.

He took hold of both of her hands, looked into her radiant face, then continued to speak, "I'm refusing to allow Elea Johnson to leave our community, as I would right here and now love to ask for her hand in marriage."

The congregation and everyone else in the fellowship hall gasped, as Kyle took a knee in front of her. His son Jack stood by his side, smiling brightly up at Elea. Kyle stared lovingly into her tear-filled eyes, reached for a small box inside of his pocket, and said, "Elea, I love you so much! Will you marry me?"

Everyone in the congregation glanced at one another with smiles of contentment on their faces. Happiness permeated throughout the entire room, and all waited in eager anticipation for her response.

Elea nodded, as she wiped a tear from her eye. Kyle then opened the box which contained a gorgeous diamond ring and slipped it on Elea's finger. He took her into his arms and passionately kissed her while everyone cheered.

Afterwards, every member of the congregation expressed congratulations and warm wishes to both of them, as well as to Jack.

The end of the month arrived. Amidst tender and emotional goodbyes, Elea hugged Scott and all of the volunteers. They had shared such wonderful memories together in the small community, having labored tirelessly in doing the Lord's work.

"I'll miss all of you, Scott," Elea shed a tear as she hugged him and wished him well, "Please stay in touch and let me know where all of you go on assignment. If Father Bud will let you come back to us in the future, I would love it, and I know this community will, too."

Scott replied, "Be well and happy, dear Elea. We arrived in this community together as part of an outreach mission, and we worked hard and fellowshipped with everyone. And you, my dear friend, found your destiny. You're going to become the wife of a church pastor, and a stepmother to a great little guy." Scott smiled and gave her one last big hug.

As Elea waved goodbye to Scott and to all of the volunteers, she considered Scott's departing words to her. Her journey in this particular community had certainly been an undeniable combination of fellowship and destiny.

Kyle and Elea married that spring. His best friend from divinity college, Brent Somerville, performed their wedding ceremony at the quaint Evangelical Community Church. Every member of the congregation was in attendance on that beautiful sunny afternoon. They came to witness the marriage of handsome Pastor

Kyle Williams and the beautiful Miss Elea Johnson. Needless to say, there was great joy resounding throughout the small church community of Scarlet Oak Valley, Tennessee.